Accidental Baby Daddy

A Single Dad Runaway Bride Romance

Unintentionally Yours

Mia Mara

**Running from the altar was just the beginning.
Now I'm back in my small hometown... running
straight into the arms of my ex.**

After ditching my fiancé in New York, I stumble into our town's bar looking like a runaway bride cliché. The last thing I needed was a cute guy offering to buy me a drink. Especially when that guy turns out to be Oliver Stanhope - the man whose heart I broke when I left, now a single dad, and somehow still managing to look ridiculously hot.

One drink leads to one wild night, and I thought that would be the end of it. But then I find out the cabin I'm renting? It's on *his* property. Now Oliver is my neighbor, plus my ex-fiancé is hot on my trail, and to top it off... I'm pregnant with Oliver's baby.

Just your average *accidental baby daddy* situation, right?

Oliver and I have some unfinished business. But if we can survive my ex, awkward small-town gossip, and this whole neighbors-with-benefits thing, maybe we can find our way to a happy ever after.

Chapter 1

Lexie

"**A**lexandra!"

The sound of my fiancé screaming my name as I bolted around the side of the church put a fire under my butt, and I pumped my muscles harder, my thighs aching.

The grass and gravel threatened to bowl me over, but I managed to stay upright, hitching the train of my ten-thousand-dollar wedding dress up around my hips to keep from tripping on it. My head was spinning, but it also felt empty.

I just needed to *run*.

When I turned to look back to make sure that Dick wasn't gaining on me, I saw that he'd given up, doubled-over and panting as I made my way to the highway. The venue was close to the airport, only about a five-minute drive. I was in great shape though running in a wedding dress was a lot different than running in workout gear.

All I knew was that I couldn't stay there. I couldn't marry Richard Whitman. Not because I wasn't in love with him, although that was one of the reasons. But because we

1

wanted different things out of life. *Much* different things. Besides, I was tired of being treated like a doormat.

The only belongings I had on me were five-hundred bucks in cash and my driver's license, both stuffed in my bra. My phone, my purse, everything else was back at the church or at Dick's house. It had never felt like my house, even though we'd been living together for almost a year.

Dick's things were Dick's things, and he didn't share. He was very clear about that.

"You can buy your own things," he'd say whenever I'd complain. He managed all the money. I worked part-time as Dick's personal assistant because I had plans to go back to school. It never happened, however, so lately I'd been looking for a full-time position.

The last time I'd seen Dick before the wedding, we'd gotten into an argument. We were always getting into arguments.

"You should stop all that job searching," he complained as I scrolled through a job site.

"Why would I do that?"

"Because I'll take care of you," he promised, kissing my cheek as if that was supposed to somehow reassure me in a romantic way.

Dick had a lot of money and always had. He was born in upstate New York and had settled in the city to play the stock market. I wasn't exactly sure what his job position entailed, but I knew it earned him a lot of zeros in his bank account—that along with the trust fund his parents had set up for him.

The Whitmans were well-known in New York. When I first began dating Dick it had seemed like dating royalty in a way.

He took me to all the fanciest places, bought me the

most expensive, beautiful jewelry. I was wearing the heart locket encrusted with diamonds that he bought me on our fourth date when I fled the church. I guess I got caught up with all the money, all the fame, definitely the financial stability.

It wasn't that I felt unwanted by Dick, it was more... transactional. For a kid who didn't feel like a priority to my parents—or anyone else in my life—there was comfort in that, regardless of the condition of our relationship.

I take that back; I suppose I was a priority to at least one person. But there was no reason to think about that now.

Oliver was another lifetime ago. I was a different person then and I'm sure he was, too. So what if Dick never made me feel like Oliver did? So what if when we were in bed he never even made me come?

Relationships aren't all sex and excitement. You have to work at them.

But there was no working on my relationship with Dick. As I was walking down the aisle, I couldn't help but think about how much Dick whined and complained, how our kids would end up having his big, stupid nose and how they'd be whiners, too.

I had to get out of there.

JFK is a huge airport and I just needed to make it to one of the gates...

I prayed while I thudded down the side of the highway, exhausted, sweating. I prayed that I had enough money for a plane ticket to Dallas, Texas, near my hometown of Wagontown.

I didn't have anywhere else to go.

Dick had made it so that I was isolated and I didn't have any friends, but at the same time, I simply hadn't made any. I moved away from Wagontown because I had to get out of my parents' house, had to get away from my little sister—the golden child. It wasn't that I didn't love my family, of course I did, but I always felt like I came second fiddle to Gillian.

I never really discussed my childhood or my homelife with Dick. He never asked where I grew up, never seemed to be interested. But at least with Dick, I felt like number one. I helped him with his work, we spent a lot of time together, even when he was busy. He'd been sweet and attentive at first, and I'd clearly been a priority in his life. So when he got down on one knee at our favorite restaurant, I'd said yes immediately, throwing my arms around him.

I thought it was what I wanted.

"What do you mean, you'll take care of me?"

He frowned, concern shadowing his brown eyes. "Of course I'll take care of you, Alexandra. You'll stay at home and keep up the house, and then, when the children come—"

"Children?"

My mouth went dry. I didn't know why I'd never thought about it, whether Dick would want kids, but I couldn't imagine him being a father. He was so... cold. Robotic, almost.

"Two or three, at least," he said, smiling, but I didn't smile back.

That wasn't the first time I'd been unsure about Dick, but it certainly gave me pause. Over the past few months, he'd grown more and more controlling. I'd gone out with coworkers a few times and he'd nearly lost his mind, calling me over and over for hours while I was out. Not only that, but when he thought it was time for me to come home, he'd lock the credit card that he'd given me to use. Luckily, I had some of my own money to cover the bill but the way he controlled everything else...

When I arrived home, he acted as if nothing happened. He was as sweet and attentive as always.

But it was another red flag.

I guess the real straw that broke the camel's back was when he talked about kids. I suddenly realized that although I'd always wanted children, I didn't want children with him. I didn't want them to be controlled the way I was controlled.

I was running out of steam when I heard the squealing of tires in the distance. Assuming it was Dick, I panicked, jumping into some nearby bushes behind a building. I hid there, panting, until I heard the car drive past, the calls of my name fading away.

I'd always preferred my nickname, Lexie, but Dick insisted on calling me by my full name, Alexandra. I used to think it was endearing but now I find it annoying and another way he uses to control me.

I slowly climbed out of the bushes, pretty sure that there were sticks and small branches stuck in my dark hair, which was braided and piled on the top of my head.

I looked at the long stretch of highway before me. I didn't know if I was going the right way because I didn't know New York City the way I knew Wagontown. I only remember seeing the airport outside the limo window when we drove from this direction to the church.

A semi honked as I stumbled out onto the road, and I yelped and jumped backwards, falling into the ditch as my heels buckled.

The next thing I knew, someone was standing over me, their shadow blocking the bright June sun. The person was tall, and for a moment, fear tightened my throat.

"Honey, you look like you've had a *day*," the woman said, and I was relieved to hear an obvious Texan accent.

"I really have," I replied, and the woman reached out her hand to help me up.

"I'm Lily. Short for Lillain, but don't tell anyone."

"Lexie," I greeted her with a small smile, brushing off my dress as I stood. "Short for Alexandra, but don't tell anyone."

Lily chuckled, jerking her head toward the semi which was parked on the shoulder of the other side of the highway. "Looks like you might need a ride."

She looked me up and down. It was obvious that I was a runaway bride—my hair and makeup done to the nines, broken heels, wearing a ridiculously expensive dress, now sullied with dirt and twigs.

"Yes, please," I breathed, relieved. "I can pay you for gas—"

"Absolutely not," she cut me off, frowning and leading me across the empty highway. "I was planning on going past the airport, anyway." She paused. "I assume you want to get the hell out of here?"

"Yes, ma'am."

"That accent..." she trailed off. "Oklahoma?"

"Texas," I said, and she broke into a huge smile that made her look ten years younger.

"My old stomping grounds. I miss it. New York is quite the culture shock for us country girls."

"You're telling me," I muttered as she opened the passenger door and helped me up into the cab.

She started up the truck and instantly cold air blew into my face. It felt so good I almost moaned. It was a particularly hot day for June, and I'd probably have one hell of a sunburn once I finally got to where I was going.

Thing was, I wasn't sure where that was. I hadn't talked to my parents in probably three years.

I was sure they'd been in touch with Gillian, though, my little sister. I guess I was hoping that my family would take me in regardless, at least for a few months until I could get back on my feet. I prayed that they would.

When Lily stopped at the next gas station to fill up, I walked inside, buying myself a bag of chips and a stick of beef jerky. I hadn't eaten since lunch yesterday; I'd been too nervous last night and this morning.

After I devoured my snacks, Lily offered me a thermos full of cold water, and I gulped greedily as if it were nectar from the gods.

By the time we arrived at the airport, I felt a lot more human.

"Are you on your way back home to Texas?" Lily asked as we approached the terminal. She hadn't spoken much on the way there. It was about a half an hour drive, so I was more than grateful that she picked me up. Although, in truth, I probably could have made it there quicker on foot.

"I am," I said, and reached into my dress, pulling out my cash. I tried to offer her some but she immediately pushed my hand away. "No need for that. I'm happy to help get a fellow Texan back home. I hope to get there myself, someday."

"If you do, look me up. Lexie Tripp of Wagontown," I told her as I jumped out of the cab. She gave me a sloppy salute and a wink.

There really are angels on Earth, and people like Lily proved that. I watched her drive away before heading into the terminal and toward the ticket booths.

The cashier didn't even blink an eye, clearly used to seeing somebody like me showing up at her station while working at JFK.

"International or domestic?"

I was able to get a one-way ticket for Dallas, thank God, and once I got through security, I wondered who I knew still living in Wagontown.

Specifically, I wondered if Oliver was still there.

Oliver Stanhope. My first love. My first heartbreak.

Surely, he wouldn't still be in town. He was probably married now with kids, he'd always wanted a family. The thought was a little bittersweet, even with how things ended with us. Nevertheless, I still wished the best for him.

Besides, the odds that I'd run into him were a million to one.

Chapter 2

Oliver

M y father looked pale and withdrawn when he opened the door, and I couldn't say I blamed him.

"How are you holding up, old man?" I asked gently, and he shrugged.

"Been better," he admitted, his voice hoarse. He had bags under his eyes, as if he hadn't been sleeping.

I walked past him into the living room of his new apartment. An empty, smelly pizza box sat on the coffee table, and I wrinkled my nose.

"Anchovies."

My father laughed. "Your mother would never let me order them."

With good reason, I thought but didn't say.

My father's penchant for smelly fish wasn't what made my mother want to separate, but it certainly didn't help. Neither did his long hours working on the oil rig.

"Trent's out in the car," I said. "Ready to go to dinner?"

He looked ready, his button-up shirt wrinkly but clean.

My father nodded, clearing his throat, and sliding on his

shoes at the door. "I appreciate you coming over to visit, Ollie. I'm sorry I'm in such a bad way."

I clapped him on the shoulder. "It's all right, Dad. It happens to the best of us."

Hell, it had even happened to me though it was a long time ago. Not after thirty years, luckily, but still. I couldn't think about Lex now, that would just send me into a spiral. I needed to be there for my dad, not wallowing in my own past hurts.

My parent's separation brought a lot of that up again, and it was hard to ignore.

When we got into my truck, Trent whooped out a cheer from the backseat.

"Grampa!"

"Hey, slugger," my father responded, his mood seeming to lift. "What have you been up to lately?"

"Coloring," he said, his l sounding like a w.

Trent was every bit of five years old, but his speech impediment sometimes made him sound younger. He had a big vocabulary for his age, but some people didn't understand that just because he had trouble with pronunciation didn't mean he was slow or underdeveloped.

The speech therapist at school assured me that some kids just take a while to catch up, and that Trent was well on his way. I found it kind of cute, but I didn't want Trent to be bullied for it, so I was relieved to know he was improving.

"Gonna be an artist, huh? Your dad used to draw, you know," my father said, humming in the back of his throat.

"Dad used to draw?" Trent asked, his blue eyes widening.

"He did. I think I may have kept some of his drawings. I'll show you when we get back."

10

"Wow, Dad," Trent said solemnly. "You're full of surprises." He was so grownup for his age.

I snorted out a laugh. "Well, don't say that until you see the drawings."

We arrived at the restaurant, a local steakhouse that I knew served a burger that Trent would actually eat. He was a picky eater, but if all the burger had was cheese and meat, he'd be okay.

The hostess smiled brightly at us before taking us to our seats, her cheeks flushing when I smiled back. I was used to getting attention from women. I wasn't egotistic, but I saw myself in the mirror every day and I knew that I was attractive.

My parents were still good-looking, even in their mid-fifties. Mom, with her dark auburn hair showing a few streaks of grey and a figure that most twenty-year-olds would envy, and Dad, with a full head of salt and pepper hair and a body that was still in good shape.

Years on an oil rig had made him broad and muscular, and he kept it up as he got older, only developing a slight belly pouch.

I ordered myself a beer yet when I tried to order Dad one, he held up a hand to stop me.

"Not drinking right now," he muttered.

"That's a good idea, Dad," I said softly, and cancelled my beer, ordering a soda instead and a juice for Trent.

I knew that my dad had the tendency to drink too much when he was upset, and I was proud of him for denying himself alcohol while he was in a bad spot.

The waitress brought our drinks, and we ordered dinner. Trent occupied himself with crayons and a couple of kid's menus, while Dad looked over at me, rubbing his hands over his thighs nervously.

"How is your mother doing?"

"Dad—" I started, but he cut me off.

"I just want to know she's okay."

"She's okay," I said softly. "She's hanging in there. She misses you."

He scoffed. "I don't know about that."

"I'm sure she does, Dad, it's just... you know Mom. She's hard to get a read on."

"Don't I know it."

My father was always the emotional, passionate one while my mother was more reserved. When she asked him suddenly for a separation, my father was floored. So was I. She wouldn't explain exactly what it was that spurred her to do it, and my father and I were both at a loss.

It could be a million things, I supposed. I didn't know the intricacies of my parent's relationship anymore. I'd been living on my own for years.

"How long have you been off the rig?" Dad asked, and I couldn't help but grin.

"Too long. I'm itching to go back."

"You know, now that you own those rigs, you don't have to physically be there all the time," my dad drawled. "That's one of the perks of being an oil magnate."

"I like being on the rigs. They keep me in shape. Keep me humble."

Dad hummed in response, but I knew he understood. After all, he owned a few rigs himself, and he'd always gone out to work whether he needed to or not. We were rough-necks through and through. It was in our blood. My grand-father, Dirk, first struck oil in nineteen-forty-five, right here in Wagontown.

Our family has lived here ever since, although Dad and I both did plenty of traveling to offshore rigs for work. I'd grown up with oil on my hands, following Dad around the rigs, going on multiple business trips with him.

I'd never done without, but I'd also learned the value of hard work. I was grateful for my dad because of that, and grateful to my mom for being gentle and sweet with me. I had great parents growing up and I still do. I'll tell anyone who asks the same.

That's one of the reasons why I'm so worried about this separation. Mom seems okay, if a little dimmed, but I know Dad is lost without her, and it shows on his face and in his actions.

"Is she seeing anyone else?" Dad blurted out, and I nearly dropped my bread.

"Dad, no," I insisted, and I really didn't think she was. I wasn't just humoring him or sparing his feelings. "She told you that's not what it's about."

"What is it about, then?" he asked, exasperation evident in his tone as he watched Trent pick apart a roll and eat it. "She won't talk to me."

"She won't talk to me either," I admitted. "But she has her reasons. Maybe she just needs some space. It'll come out in time."

"I miss her."

I reached across the table to take my father's hand in mine, squeezing it softly.

"I know you do, Dad. Things will work out. You'll see."

Tears filled his brown eyes, so much like mine, but they didn't fall.

"All right, son. Maybe you're right."

Trent began chatting with his grandfather about a new friend he'd made at school, and Dad teased him about having a girlfriend, even though Trent insisted the little girl, Holly, wasn't his girlfriend but only a *girl* who was a *friend*.

13

I watched them, smiling fondly, as the food arrived.

I dug into my ribeye, loving the way the blood dripped from the meat as I put it on my fork.

Trent grimaced. "Gross, Dad."

"Delicious," I insisted, stuffing my mouth full as he glared at me, slowly eating his burger.

Dad laughed and it sounded genuine. I smiled at him, hoping that this outing was making him better and perhaps a little more connected to family.

As an only child, I was all my parents had until Trent.

"What are your plans for the rest of the night?" I asked. Dad just shrugged, which seemed to be a common answer from him lately.

"Probably just watching television. Being retired isn't all it's cracked up to be."

"You could go out with me. We don't have to order alcohol; we could just go somewhere and have fun."

Dad scoffed. "What kind of fun? None of those club girls want an old man sullying their experience."

"You're not old, Dad."

"Tell that to my joints," he joked, and I chuckled.

"Grampa is old," Trent said. "But so is Dad."

"Ouch," I replied, dramatically putting my hand over my heart. "Harsh, kiddo."

Trent shrugged. "It's true."

My father laughed, long and loud, and it sounded like it came from his gut. It made my heart happy to hear him laughing with us. I knew that he'd been having a really hard time. Thirty years, gone, in the blink of an eye.

I couldn't imagine. With what I went through with Lex, it would have broken me to have been with her for that long only to lose her.

Dad seemed to be in better spirits as we left the restaurant.

"Are you sure that you don't want to go out?"

"I'm sure," he grunted as he got out of the truck. Trent slept peacefully in the backseat, his head against the cushion of his car seat.

Dad opened the back door to kiss him goodbye, and Trent hugged him tightly before going right back to sleep. Dad smiled, fondness and love glowing in his brown eyes.

"See you soon, Dad," I said, watching him as he unlocked the door of his apartment.

It was a small place, not much to it, but I supposed he was hoping that he wouldn't be there for long. With the money my father had, you'd think he'd have a penthouse apartment or something bigger, nicer.

But he'd never wanted anything other than the three-bedroom home he'd bought with Mom.

I owned a six-bedroom house that was more of a mansion, but then again, I'd kind of gone buck wild when I made my first million. Sometimes I regretted it, having so much space for just me and Trent. But most of the time I loved it, especially my heated indoor pool and in-home theater.

If you had it, why not spend it and flaunt it? That was my philosophy.

I headed next to my childhood home. When I arrived, my mother was seated on the front porch in one of the rocking chairs. It hurt my heart to see her rocking with no one in the seat next to her, so once I got Trent inside and in his bed, I came out to sit next to her.

She smiled at me. "How did dinner go?"

That was probably her way of asking how Dad was.

"He's... struggling, Mom."

"We're all struggling," she mumbled, looking away, but not before I spotted hurt in her blue eyes.

"What's going on with you and Dad?" I asked. "Why did you ask him to leave?"

She sighed. "It's complicated, Ollie. Trent staying the night?"

Of course, she'd change the subject. It was her go-to when she didn't want to talk about something. And if Mama didn't want to talk, I knew better than to press her.

"If it's all right with you. Thought I'd meet up with a friend for a beer or three."

She smiled and nodded. "That's good. You need to get out more. Stop working so much."

I leaned over to kiss her cheek. "Thank you for looking out for Trent."

She waved her hand at me. "He's my only grandson. You know I'll always look out for him."

I smiled and stood up, walking slowly to the truck, and getting in.

Even though my dad declined my invitation, I was feeling restless. I needed to get out, needed to let loose. Mom was right—it had been too long.

Something felt different in the air tonight. Maybe if I went out, I'd end up having a really good time, good enough to get my mind off everything for a little while. It felt like something was coming, I could feel it in the hair on the nape of my neck.

Something good was happening in the air, and I wanted to be there for it. Whatever it was.

Chapter 3

Lexie

When I arrived in Dallas, I realized that the only phone number I had was my sister's, and I was loath to call her. At least not yet.

Instead of calling her from one of the few remaining pay phones in the airport, I went to the gift shop and bought myself one of those prepaid phones. It took nearly the rest of my money, but it would come in handy.

I neglected to buy myself some clothes because it was either the clothes or the phone. By the time I took a very expensive taxi to Wagontown I was sweating, with only a wrinkled five-dollar-bill to my name tucked in my bra.

As the taxi pulled away, I stood in the quiet heart of my hometown, the soft glow of streetlights illuminating the familiar scene. Main Street looked much the same, the old diner's neon sign flickering and the vintage movie theater marquee advertising a double feature. The scent of jasmine from Mrs. Thompson's garden filled the air, mixed with the distant hum of cicadas. Shadows played on the worn facades of the quaint shops, each one a piece of my childhood. Despite the years I'd been gone, it felt like

17

Wagontown had been holding its breath, waiting to welcome me back.

I knew I should call my sister but I didn't know if I could bring myself to do it. Gillian was six years younger than me, and my parents had always favored her.

And why wouldn't they? She was the golden child. She got good grades and did well in sports, while I hid inside books, always escaping to fantasy worlds and getting by with a C average. I had started to work harder from the moment she was born, wanting my parent's affection, aching for it, fighting for it. But it didn't work. Although I was doing better, that was what I was expected to do, so my efforts were often overlooked.

And I resented her for it. I really did. It wasn't fair, but I couldn't help it.

I tucked my new phone into the small pocket of my wedding dress' skirt and started to walk. I didn't know where I was going until the Pig in the Poke came into view.

God, so many memories there. I'd thrown up in that bathroom too many times to count whenever I got too drunk, my friends holding my hair.

Friends that I hadn't talked to in years.

I walked inside and began looking around before I knew what I was doing.

The pool table where Oliver had first kissed me. The end of the bar, where Oliver had ordered us a round of cheap tequila shots and we had almost spit them out. It made me a little sad yet nostalgic at the same time. Some part of me almost expected to see him here, but surely he wouldn't still be around.

I walked up to the bar and chuckled as the bartender's eyes widened.

I knew I looked a mess, my makeup streaking from

sweat, my very expensive wedding dress wrinkled and dirty, pieces of my hair sticking out of the braid it was in with tendrils falling over my face.

I huffed the hair out of my face and awkwardly put myself on the bar stool, stuffing my dress beneath me.

"I really need a drink but I only have five bucks. Any way there's a happy hour so I can get a shot?"

The bartender winced and shook her head. "Unfortunately not but I could get you a beer?"

I nodded gratefully and slid her the wrinkled, damp bill that I took out of my purse. "Keep the change. If there is any."

She smiled. "What's your poison?"

"Anything light."

"I'm Brenda," she told me, sliding the beer to me.

I took a long sip, instantly grateful I got beer rather than a shot. I was thirsty, and a shot wouldn't have helped that.

"Lexie," I told her, and it felt strange to say that after having been Alexandra for so long.

"Nice to meet you, Lexie. Where you from? Not around here, I'd wager."

Brenda had long dark hair, a touch of grey around the temples. I guessed her to be in her forties. She was friendly and very attractive. I bet she made great tips.

"You'd be wrong," I said, taking another long sip of my beer. "I'm from Wagontown. But you are not."

"I'm a city gal, myself."

"How did you end up here? It's barely on the map."

She shrugged. "I followed a roughneck here, because of the oil rig."

I nodded slowly. My ex-boyfriend, Oliver, had been a roughneck in high school and college. His father was an oil magnate, and Oliver had been on his way to following in his footsteps. "I've known a few of them myself."

"They're hot," she said with a wink, and I couldn't help but laugh. I had hardly eaten all day and the beer was already going to my head. I was a little bummed when I finished it.

People started to come in, and I looked down at my wedding dress, feeling embarrassed.

Brenda eyed me and then passed me a pair of kitchen scissors.

"Thank you," I whispered, and went to the bathroom to hack up my ten-thousand-dollar dress. By the time I was finished, it barely resembled its original form—no sleeves, the hem hanging just below my knees.

I took a deep breath and headed back out to the bar. Brenda whistled at me and winked, and I couldn't help but smile.

That was one of the great things about Wagontown. There were good people here.

I was about to ask Brenda if I could owe her five bucks for another beer when a man walked up behind me.

"Put whatever she wants on my tab," he said. Grateful, I turned and looked up at him.

My heart stopped in my chest before booming back to life again and beating way too hard. I felt dizzy, as if I'd been taking shots all night instead of nursing one light beer.

This wasn't happening. This couldn't be happening. It had to be some fantasy I'd made up because I was stressed about pulling a runaway bride. I closed my eyes tightly and tried to push the fantasy away. But when I opened them seconds later, he was still standing there. Oliver Stanhope, the only man I had ever loved, stood there, looking at Brenda.

Did he recognize me? Or was he just being nice to the crazy lady in the cut up wedding dress?

"Oliver," I whispered, and he looked down at me, frowning, before realization dawned in his soulful brown eyes.

"Shit," he whispered back. "Lex."

He looked good, great, even. Chiseled jaw with a hint of dark stubble across it. Those big brown eyes I used to get lost in were still the same. He was broader across the chest and shoulders than the last time I'd seen him, but of course, it had been years.

He smelled good, too, like sandalwood and soap. God, I still wanted him. I swallowed hard and looked up at him.

"God, it's been a long time," I babbled, not sure what else to say. I felt like my knees would buckle if I tried to stand up.

Oliver slid onto the bar stool next to me. "What are you doing back in town?" He eyed my outfit with one dark brow lifted in inquiry.

I reflected that this was one of the things I had always liked about him. He didn't panic or make a big to-do about anything. Even running into his ex in what was left of her wedding gown with sticks in her hair.

I gestured down to my wedding dress. "Running," I admitted ruefully, one corner of my mouth lifted a little. Suddenly, I felt tears prickling in my eyes, and I looked away from him. What was wrong with me?

He chuckled. "You were always good at that."

I frowned, but Oliver didn't seem angry. Maybe he'd forgiven me after all this time. I'd forgiven him, not that this was the time or the place to say so.

"No hard feelings?" I asked, and he shrugged.

"I guess there's no hard feelings," he admitted. "Are you

back or just passing through?" He gave my outfit another significant glance.

He was looking at me curiously, and I wondered if he was being honest about not having hard feelings or if he was just saving face.

The last time we'd seen each other we'd both been screaming and highly emotional. It seemed strange now that everything appeared to be okay.

I guess people could change. I guess time changed things too. Time had made me foolish, apparently, and time had made him wise. I sighed.

I hailed Brenda for another beer and Oliver ordered himself one too. I took a long sip before speaking again.

"Yeah. Wanted to look up my parents."

"I hate to tell you this, Lex, but they moved away. East coast, somewhere."

I swallowed hard. "Damn."

I wasn't sure how to feel about that. Why wouldn't they have at least called to tell me? I guess that just further proved what a black sheep I was.

"I take it you haven't kept in touch with them or Gilly?"

I shook my head. "Just... drifted apart, I guess."

"Your sister still lives in town. You can look her up."

Shit. That was what I was hoping I wouldn't have to do. As much as I loved my baby sister, she got everything handed to her that I had to work so hard for. It was tough to be around that all the time. I almost wanted to cry again.

"I guess so."

"Do you want a ride?" Oliver asked, and I blinked at him.

"You'd give me a ride to my sister's place?" I stared at him for a long moment. Why was he being so nice to me after everything that happened between us?

He shrugged. "If that's what you want."

I looked up at him curiously. "What's the alternative?"

Oliver gave me a small smile, showing a dimple in his cheek that I used to love.

"You could go to a hotel. We could catch up, wings and beer, like we used to."

"You want to catch up?"

He shrugged again. "We said no hard feelings, didn't we?" But there was something in his eyes that I couldn't quite name, something hot and resentful.

"I don't know," I mused. "I don't have a cent to my name."

"I'll spot you the cash," Oliver said, adding, "what are friends for?"

"Come on," Brenda said from behind the bar. "He's gorgeous."

"Thank you, Brenda," Oliver replied, and she winked at us. I suppose Oliver did come to the Pig every now and again, they seemed to know each other.

But then again, everyone knew each other in Wagontown.

I gave him a once-over. He clearly still worked out. His biceps and pecs bulged slightly in the t-shirt he wore. Oliver had always had money, but he dressed casually. He wasn't a suit person, even though he looked great in one.

He now wore his brown hair a little past his collar, and I wondered briefly what it would be like to run my fingers through it again.

I cleared my throat. "I'd love to, thank you," I muttered. Even though I had my issues with Oliver and how things had ended, I needed this. I needed to let loose, and as much as I was loath to admit it, his presence gave me a sense of security.

I didn't want to talk about Dick and why I was back in Wagontown with nothing to my name in my torn-up wedding dress. It was embarrassing, to say the least, and a little traumatic if I really delved into how I was feeling. Oliver didn't even ask, instead leading me to a nearby table and ordering from the waitress.

"Can I ask where you moved to?"

"New York City," I told him.

He whistled. "Big city girl. You always wanted to get out of Wagontown."

I hummed. That wasn't exactly true. I'd always wanted to get away from my family but never away from Oliver. Sure, I'd had dreams that Oliver and I would get married and settle down in another city, another state. But Oliver had always wanted to stay right where he was born—in Wagontown.

"It wasn't all it's cracked up to be. The big apple is kind of rotten if you know what I mean."

He laughed, nodding. "I've been there. It's a lot different than out here under the open sky."

"What about you?" I asked, looking over at him. "Have you always stayed in Wagontown?"

"Yep," he said easily. "Built myself a house and settled in."

I wondered why he had chosen to say, 'settled in' and not 'settled down.' Did that mean that he wasn't married?

"I'm not surprised."

"I never wanted to get out the way you did."

"I know," I said gently, thinking about our second to last fight which had been about me applying to graduate school at New York University.

As I looked around the Pig, I realized that I didn't know I was homesick until right then.

24

Not that I wanted to move back. I should have visited more though.

"Miss it?" he asked me, his gaze perceptive.

I swallowed hard. Yes. "Not really," I lied, but then I started crying for real. So much for what was left of my makeup.

"Liar," he said to me. He didn't pull me in for the hug I would have liked to have, but he did pass me some napkins off the bar.

"I feel so stupid," I sniffled. "I did everything right."

He winged a brow at me. "Right? What does that mean? There's not really rights and wrongs when it comes to life."

I just shook my head. I had always thought there were. Until recently, that is.

I couldn't help but wonder if this was fate, bringing us back together.

Chapter 4

Oliver

I was not going to have a panic attack because Lexie Tripp walked back into my life in a dirty wedding dress. I was fine. Absolutely fine.

I just couldn't seem to breathe very well, and I was inwardly freaking out.

What had I been thinking, sitting next to her, and ordering her a beer? What the hell had happened to her, and how did she end up here? I hadn't pushed, telling myself it was none of my business, but I was curious.

Who was this guy she had been about to marry? Was he good looking? Was he taller than me? Better than me in bed? I had a million questions swirling around my head, but I didn't want to know the answers to any of them.

What if she planned to go back to him? God, this was such a bad idea. Not to mention that I'd told her no hard feelings and that was a lie. What happened between us had broken me, but I wasn't about to show her that. I wanted her to think I cared as little as she did.

I huffed out a breath and she tilted her head, looking at me curiously. I checked my phone to appear disengaged.

"You have a hot date?" she asked, and I noted there was no edge to her voice. She was over it. Over me. And I was over her.

No big deal.

I smiled. "No, nothing like that. Just wondering if I can start drinking liquor."

She laughed. "It's after five o'clock."

"Exactly."

I ordered a tequila and pineapple from the bartender, and she ordered the same.

"Still your favorite drink?" she asked, smiling up at me. God, she was beautiful. She'd always been the most beautiful woman in the world to me, and it seemed like nothing had changed.

But I was different. I was over her. I could do this, talk to her like an old friend who I had absolutely no lingering feelings for.

"Always."

She shrugged. "It's a good go-to."

"You have a new favorite?"

She grinned. "Dirty martini. Correction—filthy martini, actually."

I raised an eyebrow. "What's a filthy martini?"

"Vodka and olive juice, shaken and chilled."

I shuddered. "That sounds awful."

"It's delicious," she argued. "In fact, I'm thinking about asking Brenda for some olives." Her stomach rumbled in the most obvious way.

When the waitress came back, I ordered wings, extra hot, just like she used to love.

"Oh, thank God," she muttered. "I'm starving."

I chuckled. "I never minded feeding you."

She smirked. "I've gained thirty pounds, so I guess I

don't mind feeding myself."

I couldn't help but look her over. "It looks good on you," I said and I meant it. I wasn't just flattering her, either. She really did look good, her hips wider, her breasts bigger. Her waist was still trim, with a belly that I bet would feel so soft under my hands. As she looked up at me with her bright green eyes, I noticed she hadn't aged at all.

I, however, had crow's feet around the corners of my eyes. I wondered if she noticed.

Lexie blushed.

"I cannot *wait* for these wings."

She seemed excited, and I couldn't help but chuckle.

"You're really psyched to be back at the Pig. Don't think I've ever seen someone so excited to be here."

"It's been too long," she said. "Does that one guy still bartend?"

"Jorge? No, he went to college, settled out in California."

"Aw, he was my favorite," she whined. "But, good for him."

This place held a lot of fond memories for me and Lexie, and I wondered if she remembered them as well as I did.

Part of me hoped she did.

A big part of me.

I didn't know where this night would end, but I felt like I'd follow her to hell if she asked me to.

I was clearly not over Lexie Tripp.

* * *

Two hours later, we'd each had a few more beers and shared some wings and fries. Lexie seemed to be having a great

28

time. I was having a great time, too, better than I'd had in years.

We were able to talk about the past without bitterness, and I was grateful for that.

"I'm glad there are no hard feelings," Lexie said, and I nodded. It made my head spin a little. Maybe that last beer had been one too many.

"Of course not," I said easily. "Why would there be?"

Because you broke my heart.

But I'd grown since then. I'd matured. I could handle my high school sweetheart, my first and only heartbreak. Couldn't I?

Besides, didn't everyone get a little nervous when they saw their first love? Maybe it was one of those things you couldn't help.

"You still make me a little weak in the knees," I admitted, and Lexie looked at me, her bright eyes just a tad glassy.

"Really?"

I nodded, feeling like my face was going to catch fire.

"You too," she replied in a quiet voice.

"You sure you don't want to talk about what happened?"

She shrugged. "There really isn't much to tell. I didn't love him, and he started to get a little... controlling."

I hummed in the back of my throat, feeling anger rising in me. "Is he dangerous?"

She shook her head. "I don't think so."

I swallowed hard. I didn't like the idea of some ex of hers following her around. "Does he know where you are?"

"No, not at all. I ran directly to the airport. He knows I'm from Texas, but there's no way he'd be able to figure out it's Wagontown."

My shoulders relaxed slightly. She was right, Wagontown wasn't even on some maps.

"What about you?" she asked. "Did you settle down with a wife? Have a couple of kids?"

I could tell that she was a little drunk by the glassiness of her green eyes. My vision was doubling a little after three tequila and pineapples.

I probably shouldn't have had so much to drink. It made me want things I shouldn't. Like wanting to grab Lex's hand, take her to the bathroom, and bend her over the sink.

I cleared my throat, trying to push away the thought.

"No wife. No kids."

I wasn't ready to tell her about Trent yet.

"Live-in girlfriend?"

I snorted out a laugh. "No. Just me."

"I can't believe a guy who looks like you hasn't met anyone special."

"Haven't been looking," I said honestly. Lex was my somebody special... and look how that turned out.

"Marriage is for the birds, anyway," she mumbled, and I smiled at her.

"I'm glad you're not upset about it."

She looked up at me warily, like she thought I was going to ask more questions, but in the end, I didn't. Of course I wanted to know, but it seemed like knowing might shatter the little bubble we were in.

It was like I was young again, young and in love, and it felt good, even if I hated to admit it to myself. Lexie absolutely inhaled the wings, getting sauce all over her fingers. Part of me wanted to lick it off. I was just staring at her, smiling like an idiot, when I heard her shout, looking over my head.

"Butch!" she cried out, and I looked over my shoulder to

see Butch Wiggins, one of my high school friends, at the door of the Pig.

He was dressed in a Pig in the Poke t-shirt, and it took me a moment to realize that he was working as a bouncer.

Lexie ran over to him, hugging him tightly, and jealousy rose in me. I walked right over, putting a hand on her lower back.

"Lexie and Oliver, as I live and breathe," Butch said dramatically. "Never thought I'd see you two again. Are you married now?"

Lexie shook her head fast enough that I thought her neck might get a cramp. "Just catching up," she said, and for a moment, I pictured our entire future, the future that she'd thrown away.

What if we had married? What if we'd settled down in our hometown, had the same friends, gone out with Butch and his girlfriend on weekends?

It could have been so wonderful.

Butch did a shot with us, and Lexie wrinkled her nose.

"It's been an incredibly long day, and I'm a little tipsy," she admitted. "I think I need to get to the hotel."

"Of course," I said quickly, exchanging numbers with Butch to keep in touch. My head was spinning a bit, too, so instead of driving, I put my keys in my pocket. "Let's walk."

Lexie nodded, leaning against me, and before I knew it, we were holding hands on our way to the hotel, staying that way during check in and in the elevator to her floor.

The woman behind the counter gave us a few sidelong glances that made me think she wanted to say something. I didn't want to break the spell of the moment, so I just shook my head slightly at her while Lexie was looking away. She widened her eyes and nodded, then mimed locking her lips and throwing away the key.

We got our room keys, and climbed into the elevator. Lexie leaned against me, her hair wafting fruity styling product smells at me. She even smelled the same.

We stumbled through the door at the same time, giggling as we played bumper cars in the small space. I reached out and steadied her so she didn't tumble onto her face, and the zing of awareness that shot up my arm was almost painful.

"We can hit up the mini bar if you're feeling snackish," I said to her to cover the lust coiling through me, and she smiled.

"You don't have to pay for everything, Oliver. I'll figure things out."

"Too late. I've already paid for tonight and tomorrow."

She frowned. "You—"

"Didn't have to do that. I know. I wanted to."

She looked up at me from under her eyelashes. "Is there anything else you might want to do?"

I stepped closer to her. "I don't know...I could think of a thing or two."

She smiled at me. I hated the sad look in her eyes. I wanted to make it go away. "I didn't get my wedding night," she said a bit grimly.

"I feel like we should talk about that," I said, stepping back a little.

She shook her head hard. "I can't talk about it. Not right now. What do you want to do?"

"You know damn well what I want to do."

I knew I shouldn't be doing this. My brain was yelling at me to push her away, to leave, but my heart... my heart wanted her. And my body. I'd always wanted her. I'd never stopped wanting her, and that was the truth I could never admit to myself.

"What if I want it, too?" she asked in a small voice, stepping closer, wrapping her thin arms around my neck, her ample breasts pressing against my chest.

"Lexie," I whispered, but it was too late, my mouth was pressing against hers. Her tongue slid between my lips, and I couldn't help but groan into her mouth.

I pushed her backward until the back of her knees hit the bed and she plopped down on it, giggling. It made my heart swoop with joy to hear her happiness.

I took off her bodice, ripping one side, eager to see her breasts bounce free, and unhooked her bra with one hand.

"You can still do that?" she gasped.

"Lots of practice," I mumbled, and she frowned and kissed me again, hungrier, more possessive. God, it was like we were teenagers again, except her body was fuller, her kisses more confident.

This was what it would have been like if it hadn't all gone to hell. Pleasure ran up and down my spine and I grew fully hard in my jeans, my cock rubbing against the material uncomfortably.

I took off her bra and threw it on the floor, watching her breasts fall into my hands. I rubbed my thumbs across her nipples, and she let out a long moan, arching her back and pressing herself closer to me.

"Jesus," I whispered. "I forgot how stacked you are."

"I haven't forgotten how big you are," she teased, and she put her hand on my waistband, unbuttoning my jeans and pulling me out of my underwear.

Her small hand wrapped around my base, and I thrust into it, groaning against her neck, kissing her there until she moaned.

"Oliver, please," she pleaded. I was never capable of saying no to her and this time wasn't any different.

I took off her skirt and panties and slid my fingers between her legs, pressing my face against her neck as I pushed a finger into her. I started with one, and then quickly added another, and she rocked her hips against my hand eagerly.

Everything was so familiar, and yet so different. It was intoxicating and also confusing. Like having a blind date with your best friend.

Cursing as my cock ached, I pulled her breasts out and popped them into my mouth, sucking slowly as I looked down at her.

Her green eyes went dark with desire as she spread her thighs, lying back on the bed and showing me herself. She had a trimmed landing strip but was otherwise bare and glistening.

As I watched, she dipped her fingers into her wetness, opening herself for me, biting her lower lip.

"Look at you," I mumbled. "My girl."

So many memories swirled in my mind. I felt a swoop of déjà vu as I looked at her most intimate self. Would she still feel the same way wrapped around my cock? Would she still make the same sweet noises as I fucked her?

I kicked off my jeans and underwear and covered her with my body. I took a beat to look into her eyes, trying to figure out if she really wanted this or was just feeling rejected and using me.

"What?" she asked me, worry furrowing her brow.

"Nothing," I said, pressing into her slowly. "It's just been a long time, and yet, it feels like yesterday."

She bit her lip as I parted her gently. She gasped as I rocked my hips slowly. She closed her eyes and whispered my name as I sheathed myself fully within her.

It was like coming home. It was like Christmas, and

birthdays, and climbing back into your own bed after a long vacation. She felt like all those things and more as I tried to hold still, resisting the urge to start pounding into her seeking my release.

"Oliver," she gasped, wiggling beneath me in invitation. "Oh my God you feel good. I forgot you were this good."

It was all I could do not to come immediately. I couldn't stop looking at her face, into her eyes. The green in them seemed more pronounced, somehow, and they were bright and shining.

She felt like heaven, and I couldn't help thrusting in and out of her before she was used to me. I tried to slow myself down to help her to get comfortable, panting a little with the effort to hold back.

She wrapped her legs around me, pressing closer. "Don't stop," she pleaded, her voice catching a little on the words.

"Fuck," I muttered. I surrendered to what my body wanted and started thrusting again. "Fuck you feel good," I groaned.

She moaned loudly, rocking her hips up with every thrust. I gritted my teeth, trying to make it last, but I wasn't sure I could.

As I kept up a slow and steady pace, she gasped and writhed beneath me.

"Ollie, I'm going to come," she moaned, and I cursed again, pumping into her faster as my own orgasm built in my lower abdomen.

When Lexie pulsed around me, I couldn't hold back anymore, thrusting hard and deep and spilling inside of her.

You're still in love with her, a voice in the back of my head warned, and I froze.

When I started to come down, I began to panic a little.

What if she broke my heart all over again? I still had a lot of feelings for her. Would she be able to smash my heart into smithereens all over again?

God, was that what we did? Make love? Was it still love, after all these years?

I pulled out and laid down next to her. She put her head on my chest like she always did, so she could listen to my heartbeat. She had always said it soothed her.

Lexie sighed happily as she laid on my chest. It felt familiar and it made my insides ache, something bittersweet forming in my throat. Was this all I would get with her? Or would she still be here when I opened my eyes?

I didn't think I'd be able to drift off, but I was asleep as soon as I closed my eyes.

I woke up to daylight streaming through the windows and the bed empty. When I sat up, I realized that her ripped top was on the floor and her skirt and my Nirvana t-shirt were gone.

Great. She'd ditched me and taken my shirt.

That was what I got for hooking up with the girl who ruined my life. I wanted to scream, to throw things around the room, but in the end, all I did was leave.

She didn't care anymore. Maybe she never did.

Chapter 5

Lexie

What the hell had I been thinking? Why would I have hooked up with Oliver Stanhope, the guy who put my heart in a blender when I was eighteen? I groaned as I rushed out of the hotel and padded barefoot down the street.

I was absolutely starving, so I decided to go into the local grocery store. Maybe if I stood near the deli looking sad, someone would buy me some chicken. The wings and fries we'd eaten last night were long gone and my stomach rumbled.

I stood quietly by the deli, thinking that I was going to have to call Gillian, as much as I didn't want to. Hers was the only phone number I'd remembered, and I hoped that it was still the right one.

I had one more night in the hotel and I did not want to see Oliver again.

I had to get the hell out of Wagontown before I got my heart broken once more.

As I stood there, an older woman peeked around the corner.

"You okay, honey?" she asked, walking toward me. As she got closer, her faded blue eyes lit up. "Is that little Alexandra Tripp?"

"Lexie," I corrected, narrowing my eyes as recognition washed over me. "Agnes?"

She smiled. "The one and only."

Oh, great. Of course the next person to recognize me in Wagontown would have to be Oliver's maternal grandmother, who he'd practically lived with during the summers.

"You look so great!" I exclaimed, and she did. Her gray hair was long and braided, and she had lost some weight.

She blushed. "You do, too. You grew up so pretty. All that dark hair!" She paused. "Are you here visiting Gilly? She just came in this morning for some steaks. I wondered what the special occasion was."

I shook my head slowly.

Suddenly, I started to feel emotional. I'd had such a long day yesterday, running from my own wedding, and then hooking up with Oliver...

Tears began to fill my eyes and I couldn't stop them from overflowing.

"Honey," Agnes said gently, leading me into a back office. "What's wrong?"

I spilled everything as I sobbed, leaving out my night with Oliver. Agnes listened patiently, an empathetic expression on her face.

"You poor thing," she said quietly. Then she stood up, leaving the room, and returning with a big plate of chicken and dumplings.

I dug in as soon as she handed me the plate. I couldn't help myself. It was delicious and comforting, creamy and soft, and it instantly made me feel better.

"I wish I could offer you a place to stay, but I live in a senior community living center, and they don't allow overnight guests," she said regretfully. "But if a job opens up at the grocery store, I'll call you." She paused. "Do you have a phone?"

I nodded, wiping at my mouth with a napkin she gave me and handing her my phone. She squinted down at it for a moment before putting on her reading glasses and entering her information. She then called herself to save my number in her phone. Pretty savvy for a seventy-year-old woman.

"Agnes, I can't pay you for this right now, but—"

She waved her hand. "I'm always happy to feed the hungry. Especially someone Ollie used to care about so much." She looked at me curiously. "Have you seen him?"

I stood, ignoring the question. "I should go. I need to call Gillian."

Agnes nodded, standing up and pulling me into a warm hug. I wanted to cry all over again.

"Thank you so much," I whispered, and she smiled at me, giving me one more squeeze before letting go.

I walked out into the parking lot, trying to get myself together before calling Gillian.

"Hello?" she answered on the third ring.

"Gilly?" I said shakily.

"Who is... oh, my God. Lexie? Is that you?"

"It's me," I said, as a hitching sob came from the other end of the line. I felt a wave of guilt rush through me.

"Lexie," she whispered. "I've been trying to find you for so long!"

"You... you have?"

"When we lost touch, I tried and tried to call you. Where are you? Are you safe?"

"I'm in Wagontown," I admitted, tears filling my eyes again. "At the Stop 'n Go. I'm in trouble, Gilly."

"I'll be there in ten minutes," she said, and promptly hung up the phone.

I sat down on the curb, watching cars drive by as I waited for Gilly. There weren't many.

As promised, Gilly pulled up in a little red Volkswagen about ten minutes later. I stood, squinting to see her through the window. She parked on the street before getting out and running to me, hugging me so tightly my ribs ached.

"Lexie," she sobbed, tears rolling down her face. Her eyes, green just like mine, were full of fondness. "I'm so happy you called."

I hadn't expected that kind of reunion and I wasn't sure how to feel. I suppose I should've been flattered but all I felt was guilt.

"Please, get in. Do you have any luggage?"

I shook my head. "It's... kind of a long story."

"Good thing we have plenty of time."

We drove to her home, which was a little two-bedroom townhouse up on the hill near the water tower. I told her everything along the way. I even told her about Oliver, unable to hold back.

"Jesus, Lex, you've had a rough couple of days."

"You're telling me," I groaned as we walked into her townhouse. It was nice, with pictures of me, Mom, Dad, and Gillian hanging up over the fireplace. I felt even more guilty upon seeing them.

"Lexie, why didn't you call me when he started acting like that? I would have sent you a plane ticket home and have picked you up from the airport."

"I didn't want to bother you," I mumbled, not able to tell

her that I'd always felt like I was in her shadow, how she'd always been the golden girl and I was the black sheep.

She stared at me, frowning. "Lex, you wouldn't have been bothering me. I would have been happy to see you, like I am now."

"I'm happy to see you, too," I lied, allowing her to give me another big hug. Maybe I shouldn't be so cruel to Gillian. After all, it wasn't her fault that she was so favored and spoiled.

She finally pulled away and headed into the kitchen, returning with two glasses of white wine.

I took my glass and sipped it gratefully.

"So what are you going to do about Oliver?"

"I don't want to talk about Oliver," I muttered. "I just want to chug this wine and go to sleep. This couch seems comfy."

"No way," Gillian argued. "I have a perfectly good bed in the guest room. It's only a twin, but—"

"It sounds wonderful," I interrupted her, finishing my wine in a couple of gulps and handing her the empty glass. She took it, smiling at me.

"I'm so glad you're home, Lex."

I didn't have the heart to tell her that I really wasn't home, not for good, anyway. Truth be told, I didn't know where home was anymore.

I thought I might struggle to fall asleep in an unfamiliar place, on a tiny, narrow bed, with feelings of guilt and shame choking me, but I found I could barely keep my eyes open as I snuggled under the covers.

As soon as I fell asleep, I instantly started to dream. Or should I call it a nightmare?

It was more like a memory.

"This isn't working," Oliver snapped. "We're always fighting, and after you did what you did—"

"I didn't do anything, Oliver!" I pleaded, clutching at his shirt. He pushed me away, his lips curling into a sneer.

"Like hell you didn't! I saw you and—"

"You don't know what you saw, Oliver. You flew off the handle like you always do, and now you're blaming me for something I didn't do!"

"You lied," Oliver said, his voice low, almost a whisper, and the hurt on his face was palpable as he looked down at me. "Just go."

"Oliver—"

"Go!" he yelled, his brown eyes filling with tears. I left, running full tilt across his parent's yard and hopping the fence, sobbing like my heart was broken, because it was.

I woke with a start. I couldn't stay here any longer than necessary. It was around six in the morning when I woke, and I knew that I had to get something going. I needed to go look for a job.

Gillian was thankfully still asleep when I woke, and I felt only a little bad about stealing a pantsuit from her clean laundry basket. She used to steal my clothes all the time when we were teens.

I was going job hunting. In a town like this, being a local meant a lot, and, well, technically I was a local. For now.

God, I had got to get the hell out of Wagontown.

Chapter 6

Oliver

I decided to drop Trent off at his little preschool summer camp before heading to the Stop 'n Go to replenish our groceries. I couldn't handle him running around the store and remember to get what was on the list at the same time.

My grandmother spotted me in the meat section and grinned at me, walking out to give me a big hug.

"You haven't been by in ages!"

I usually have Peter, my personal assistant, run errands like this but lately I've been feeling restless. Ever since Lexie and I hooked up I've been feeling stir-crazy, though I can't say why.

Maybe it's because I almost allowed myself to slip back into old feelings, allowing the potential of losing myself to happen all over again.

"Sorry, Granny. I'll have to come by more often," I said, kissing her cheek and giving her a big hug back, picking her up off her feet.

She giggled like a schoolgirl. "Well, what about Lexie Tripp being back in town?"

I gaped at her. "You know Lexie's here?"

She nodded. "She came by just starving, poor thing. You know she left her man at the altar. Ran right across the street and hitched a ride with a trucker."

I blinked. "She told you that?"

"She told me everything. Poor gal was all to pieces," she said. "Wish I could help her."

I thought about Lexie, wondering where she was, thinking about her penniless and with only the clothes on her back. Guilt rushed through me. As much as she'd hurt me, I didn't want her to have to struggle. I'd once loved her, after all, and still held some feelings for her... whatever they were.

"Granny, weren't you just saying you needed to replace the girl behind the deli?"

"Oh, Samantha? Yes, she's terrible," she complained. "Plus, she's leaving for college soon so we won't have her anymore once summer's over."

"Why don't you call Lexie and offer her the position?" I suggested, and Granny's blue eyes widened.

"That's such a good idea, Oliver. I did mention that if anything opened I would let her know."

"And while you're at it," I said, then paused, asking myself if I really wanted to speak my thought aloud. "You could offer her the cabin to stay in."

"What do you want for rent?"

I shook my head. "Nothing."

The 'cabin' was a three-bedroom house at the back of my property. It had already been there when I built my place, and I suppose I'd left it there out of some sense of nostalgia. It was a nice little cabin, and I used it as a guest house.

Granny smiled slyly. "You're still sweet on that girl, aren't you?"

"Granny, please," I mumbled, grabbing the rest of what I needed. "Just do it, okay?"

"All right," she said, before grabbing my hand and squeezing it. "You're a good man, Oliver."

I smiled and squeezed it back before heading to the checkout.

When I picked up Trent from his summer camp, he sighed heavily as he got in the car. "What's wrong, pal?"

"Girl troubles," he muttered, and I couldn't help but laugh.

"At your age?"

"Her name is Shelby, Dad! She's so nice." He nearly yelled the words.

"What if I told you that you can't have a girlfriend until you're sixteen?"

"That's not fair. Lots of kids at camp have girlfriends. Some guys have *two*."

I laughed, unable to stop myself.

Trent was as good-looking as his mother and sometimes, just as flirty. Suzanne Winters had breezed into my life five years ago and then breezed right out. We'd only been together a handful of times, and it was never anything serious.

I didn't hear from her for over a year until Trent got dropped off on my doorstep. She had put the legal paperwork signing away her rights away as a parent in the baby carrier along with a note that said: *You'll be better at this than I will.*

I guess Suzanne was right. I am pretty good at this. Trent is happy and healthy, and he's brought so much joy into my life. I can't even be angry at her because he's all I ever needed.

"Well, what's the problem, then?" I asked, teasing just a little.

"She doesn't like me. She said I have a big head."

I snorted but managed not to laugh out loud that time.

"You may have to let that one go, then, kid," I said sympathetically. "What do you say we eat ice cream tonight?"

"With peanuts?"

"Definitely with peanuts. And chocolate syrup."

Trent perked up after that, and later that night, while we were eating ice cream, he leaned against me.

"I love you, Daddy," he said quietly, and my heart swelled. I love Trent more than I've ever loved anyone.

"I love you, pal," I told him, kissing the top of his head. He fell asleep before the movie we were watching was over.

Granny called about ten minutes later, presumably to tell me how the conversation with Lexie went. I felt oddly nervous when her name popped up on my phone screen.

"I offered her the cabin. And a job."

"Did she take both offers?"

"Oh, she was overjoyed," Granny said quickly. "Don't worry, I didn't tell her it was your idea. But she did insist on paying rent once she gets on her feet."

"I'm glad she accepted," I muttered.

"Why didn't you marry that girl? You two were like peas and carrots growing up." She was right, we were. We were practically attached at the hip everywhere we went.

Until... well, until it all went sideways.

"Young love doesn't always last, Granny."

"I guess you're right about that."

"I should go. Keep me updated on how she's doing. I'll stay away from the cabin, so she doesn't put two and two together and figure out it's on my property."

"All right. I love you, Ollie."

"I love you, too, Granny," I said warmly, hanging up the phone. I let out a long sigh of relief. I was glad that Lexie had somewhere to call home, even if it was most likely temporary. From the way she talked the other night, it didn't sound like she was staying in town long. I knew she would be happy to get away from her sister again and get back on her feet. It was only a matter of time before she left.

Would it break my heart? Maybe. I couldn't say that it'd ever officially mended after she left, to be honest.

I saw him sometimes around town, the guy who helped ruin my life. Tristan Scott. He'd been my best friend until... well.

Until.

But I couldn't think about that. I needed to focus on helping Lexie Tripp so that she could get the hell out of town and out of my life. For good.

Sleeping with her had been a slip. A big one. But I wasn't going to let myself fall back in love. If I did that, there was no guarantee that what happened when we were younger wouldn't happen again.

I glanced out the window, seeing my Granny pull up with Lexie, giving her a tour of the cabin. At one point, Lexie glanced up at my house and I froze, but I didn't think she could spot me in the window from that far away.

Granny distracted her and quickly led her into the cabin.

Lexie Tripp was going to be living just a few hundred yards away. That should probably worry me more than it did, but I had to admit that I wanted to see where things went.

Lexie was like a drug to me, and I'd relapsed.

Only time would tell how long it would be before everything went topsy turvy all over again.

Chapter 7

Lexie

I was more than grateful to get the call from Oliver's grandmother. She assured me that the family that lived in the mansion up the hill kept to themselves, and I wouldn't have to worry about them.

Honestly, I didn't care one way or another. Having a place of my own that wasn't my sister's house was all I needed.

"You know you can stay here as long as you like," Gillian said when I told her I was moving into the cabin.

"I know," I said gently. "I just don't want to cramp your style."

She snorted. "What style? I just work, eat, and sleep."

"Well, you should be able to do that in peace," I insisted.

Gillian looked at me for a long moment. "Do you need some money? For clothes? For work?"

I swallowed hard, hating to admit that I did. "I can get by."

She shook her head and pulled out a credit card. "There's a three-hundred-dollar limit on this one," she said. "Get whatever you need."

"I'll pay you back," I promised, but Gillian shook her head.

"Being able to see you is payment enough, Lex."

I wished that I could say I felt the same way. Gillian didn't understand because she'd grown up so close to our parents, getting any and everything she wanted. I'd be close to them too if they treated me the way they treated her.

But they hadn't treated us the same way. They'd tossed me to the side as soon as Gillian was born, and I knew that wasn't her fault. But it became hard for me to be around her, watching her get everything I felt I needed and deserved.

My parents seemed incapable of loving both children. But I didn't say any of that to Gillian. Instead, let her take me to the local department store. I picked out a few pairs of black slacks and several white t-shirts, since that was the dress code at the grocery store.

I also picked up a pair of shoes, some toiletries, sandwich meat and bread, and a bottle of white wine.

"The wine might be going a little overboard," I complained, but Gillian snorted.

"It's very important, after the week you've had."

The total came to one-hundred and seventy-five dollars, meaning I'd blown through over half of her credit card limit.

I winced but Gillian didn't bat an eye.

"At least let me feed you before she comes to pick you up," she'd said.

I nodded slowly, and Gillian ordered pizza. Once it arrived, she sat in the living room and ate with me.

"How long are you going to be in town?" she asked, and I paused for a long moment.

"Just until I'm back on my feet."

She hummed. "Have you ever thought about moving back here? For good?"

"God, no!" I exclaimed, and Gillian looked a little hurt. "Not because of you, Gilly. But you know how it went down with Oliver..."

"Yeah," she said quietly. "You were so torn up about it for months."

Years, I thought but didn't say. Sleeping with Oliver Stanhope after all this time had been one of the worst decisions I'd ever made. I've been avoiding him like the plague ever since.

I refused to admit that it had felt entirely right while it was happening. I just knew that I couldn't let him lure me back to this tiny little town. I wouldn't have a future here and I didn't need to run from one man who was a mistake to another.

I wondered if he knew I was staying in his grandmother's cabin. I assumed she owned the place, since she had offered it to me.

Gillian gave me a big hug before Agnes picked me up and I returned it with a smile. She wasn't so bad after all, especially now that she was all grown up.

"I'll come back and visit," I promised, and Gillian nodded.

Agnes was chatty on the way to the cabin which was located on the outskirts of Wagontown. She talked about her store and gossiped some about Samantha, the girl that was leaving for college and I was replacing.

"She just can't keep it together, poor thing," Agnes said as we pulled up to the cabin, which was absolutely beautiful.

Recessed lighting outlined the underlip of the rooftop, making it appear warm and inviting.

"This is so nice," I breathed. I glanced up the hill where a massive house sat and noticed the outline of a man standing in a second-floor window. I frowned. "The people up the hill—"

"They keep to themselves. You won't have to worry." She said quickly.

I nodded, but I wasn't sure I liked living so close to someone else. Oh well, I couldn't look a gift horse in the mouth. Agnes insisted I didn't have to pay rent for a while, at least the first three months.

I planned to be out of here in three months.

"The kitchen and fridge are furnished with some staples," she said. "And everything works, far as I know."

"It's beautiful. Thank you so much for this, Agnes. You don't know how much it means to me, what a huge help it is."

She smiled. "Well, any friend of Oliver's is a friend of mine."

I didn't tell her we weren't exactly friends. Not anymore.

"I'll get out of your hair," she said, patting me on the shoulder. "Call me if you need anything, and don't forget your shift starts at eight in the morning. Don't be late!"

"Of course not."

After she left, I looked around, peering into the huge backyard. It was a cozy log cabin with two bedrooms. It felt warm and homey in a way I couldn't quite put my finger on.

It was too warm to run the fireplace and besides, the air conditioning felt great on my bare skin after a hot shower. I sat in the living room, sipping wine, and enjoying feeling relaxed.

I didn't even think about Oliver. At least, not much.

* * *

The Stop 'n Go was close enough that I could walk to it, and it only took me about twenty minutes. I arrived around seven-forty-five. I hadn't wanted to risk being late.

It wasn't Agnes who met me at the door but a younger woman instead, probably about Gillian's age.

"You must be the new girl," she said, smiling warmly, and I nodded, smiling back.

"Lexie."

"I'm Jessica. I'm the manager here. I'll show you the ropes."

The job was simple and straightforward—stocking inventory, taking care of customers, and running the cash register. I'd worked in retail when I was in college, so it wasn't difficult to get the hang of it.

A couple of hours later, I was stocking milk in the back when a man opened the refrigerator door to grab a gallon. We immediately locked eyes.

As soon as that bright, blue gaze settled on me I instantly recognized him.

"Lexie?" he gasped.

"Tristan," I greeted, managing a half-smile. Things hadn't gone well the last time we'd seen each other, but that hadn't been Tristan's fault. It had been Oliver's.

I walked around to greet him, and he pulled me into a quick hug.

"It's so good to see you! I thought you got the hell out of this town."

"I did," I admitted. "It just didn't exactly stick. I'm only back for a little while."

He smiled. "I always wanted to reach out. I hate the way things went for you and me... and Oliver."

I shook my head. "Let's not talk about that right now," I suggested, my heart aching just thinking about it.

"Tell me how you've been."

"I've been up and down," I admitted. "What about you? Are you married? Kids?"

"Nah. Maybe someday. Elena and I talk about it once in a while. We should catch up soon. Maybe meet for dinner and drinks sometime," he replied.

I pulled my phone out of my back pocket. "Give me your information. Getting together sounds great."

It was time for Tristan and me to heal from what had happened all those years ago.

"Have you spoken to Oliver?"

I froze. "Not much," I said vaguely. "What about you? Have you kept in touch over the years?"

Tristan shook his head. "Not at all. Didn't want him to tear my head off."

"He never should have—"

"We don't need to talk about it," Tristan said quickly, and I realized that he didn't want to reminisce about that awful day any more than I did.

"I should get back to work," I said softly, and Tristan nodded, giving me another quick hug.

"I'll keep in touch."

It would be good, seeing Tristan and Elena. We'd been in classes together in high school but I hadn't known her very well. I remember she had been beautiful then, with long red hair and bright green eyes.

I was happy for him but living in Wagontown was going to be difficult. My past kept coming back to haunt me, and I wasn't sure how much longer I could stay without getting wrapped up in it all over again.

Chapter 8

Oliver

A big part of me wanted to go by the Stop 'n Go to see Lexie, to ask her why she'd run off the other night, but I couldn't bring myself to do it. It would just stir everything up all over again.

I didn't have much to do over the next week, since my latest oil rig had just struck oil. It was mostly paperwork and phone calls, which I could do from home. I kept Trent in summer camp, though, just in case I'd have to travel during the day.

I'd been thinking about buying a couple of local businesses for some extra income—maybe for Trent's trust fund. It wasn't that I didn't already have money in the bank. I just wanted Trent to have something of his own and giving him a business would teach him some life skills and the value of a dollar.

I'd grown up understanding the meaning of hard work, and I wanted Trent to as well, even if he decided not to go into the oil business.

The Pig in the Poke was a bar I was thinking about buying, mostly because I knew the owner, Clayton, and knew he was looking to sell. He was getting on in years and was tired of bartending and being an owner.

I walked into the establishment around three in the afternoon, when they functioned more like a diner-style restaurant. There was a good rush of people there. I wondered if I did end up taking it over whether I'd focus more on the restaurant and less on the bar.

I walked up to the bartender, a young girl with big brown eyes and facial piercings. She blinked as she looked up at me, blushing a bit, and I couldn't help but grin.

I might be older now, but it was still flattering to have young girls attracted to me.

"What's your name? Haven't seen you around here before."

"Krista," she answered. "I just started about a week ago."

"You seem like you're doing a great job. Listen, honey, is Clayton around?"

She flushed deeper when I called her honey. "I think he's out grabbing supplies. He should be back soon."

I nodded. "I'll wait for him," I said, knowing I could call Agnes and she would pick up Trent from camp and keep him for as long as I needed.

I ordered a beer, nursing it as I idly flirted with Krista. There wasn't anything behind it. I wasn't interested in another fling, not after what happened with Suzanne.

I'd slept with other women since, but I always kept it casual with no strings attached, and always with protection. It dawned on me that I didn't bother to use protection with Lexie, but surely she would have told me if she wasn't on birth control.

I didn't have too much time to think about it because soon I spotted another blast from the past—Tristan. My mouth twisted into a sneer as I watched him walk through the door, and I couldn't stop myself from getting up and bumping into his shoulder—hard.

"Hello, Ollie," Tristan said dryly, glaring at me.

"I thought I told you to stay out of here," I hissed. This place was the very place I'd seen him last, when my fist connected with his jaw.

"You really have to let it go, man."

"Let what go? I thought you said nothing happened?" I shot back.

"It *didn't*, Oliver."

I scoffed. I knew better. I'd seen it with my own eyes.

I figured that Tristan would walk away. I'd seen him in town before, and I had to admit I was constantly trying to start something, but he always just shook his head and walked away.

But this time, he didn't.

"Lexie's back in town, you know."

I narrowed my eyes, anger rising in me. "How the hell do you know that? Stay away from her."

"You don't get to tell me to do that. She's not yours anymore, Ollie. You threw that all away."

"You took her from me," I burst out. I considered hitting him, but I knew if I did, Clayton would never let me buy the bar.

"Oliver?" Krista, the young bartender, called.

I turned my head, taking in a deep breath.

"Clayton is waiting for you in his office."

Shit. That could mean that he'd seen the confrontation with Tristan.

I took in another breath before walking into Clayton's office. He sat behind the desk, looking at me with questioning eyes.

"You almost started a fight in my bar."

"Look, Clayton, it's—"

"I know the story," he said gruffly. "I was here when it happened." He paused. "If I were you, I'd hit him, too."

I smiled a little at that, sitting down across from him. "I'd like to put down an offer on the Pig."

"I have a few conditions," Clayton said.

I tilted my head, curious. "Like what?"

"You don't change the name. And you don't fire my staff."

Clayton was serious about that, and I knew it. He picked his staff carefully, and almost everyone that worked at the Pig had been there five plus years. Most more than a decade. Krista was a new hire but that was rare.

"Wouldn't dream of it. The Pig is known all over for being the best diner/dive bar combo in Wagontown."

Clayton laughed. "The *only* diner/dive bar in Wagontown."

"Exactly. And you have a great staff and reputation."

He nodded. "Write up an offer, and email it to me, yeah?" He slid a business card across the desk and I took it, putting it in my wallet. "And Oliver?"

"Yeah?"

"You really should let it go. It's been, what, nearly ten years?"

I nodded, swallowing hard. He was right. I should let it go. Even Tristan was right—Lexie wasn't mine anymore. Heck, she really hadn't ever been mine.

I walked out of the bar, not spotting Tristan again. He'd always been a coward, never owning up to what he did.

I called Peter, my personal assistant, and he answered on the first ring.

"Hey, boss."

"I want to buy the Pig in the Poke," I told him. "Send over an email to Clayton Huggins. I'll send you his business card."

"Offer above asking price?"

"Always."

"All right. Anything else?"

I paused. "You want to go out for dinner?"

It was nearing six in the evening and I was starving. I hadn't eaten since breakfast.

"Sure," he said easily. "Where?"

"How about Hart's Cafe? They've got a great French dip."

"Meet you there," he said, and I headed to the cafe, thinking that Peter was probably the closest thing I had to a true friend these days.

Peter showed up just a few moments after I sat down and ordered my French dip. He sat across from me and ordered one for himself.

"You never invite me out," Peter said suspiciously. "What's going on with you?"

I shrugged. "Nothing. We're friends, aren't we?"

"Colleagues, at best," Peter said flatly.

I put a hand over my heart dramatically, as if I was hurt by his statement.

Peter laughed. "I've been working with you for what, eight years? And you've only asked me out to dinner maybe a handful of times. Mostly business related."

"Not tonight," I promised, dipping my sandwich after the server put it down on the table.

"So this is a friendly dinner?"

"Very friendly," I replied, pausing while I chewed, then letting out a breath through my nostrils. "Fine. I don't really have friends, and I needed to talk to someone."

Peter raised his eyebrows. "And you chose me?"

"Why not?" There was an edge of defense to my voice.

"Well, because I'm your employee. You really don't have any friends? That seems unlikely."

"Not really," I admitted. "My best friend in high school... well, we had a big falling out. And things are starting to resurface."

"What happened?"

I sighed. "He tried to steal my girlfriend."

"And you can't forgive him?"

"Of course not."

"You were kids, right?"

"Eighteen, nineteen," I defended, as if that wasn't considered still a kid.

He snorted out a laugh. "I was an asshole when I was that young. Weren't you?"

"Well, yes, but..." I trailed off. Peter wouldn't understand. It wasn't like Lexie was some fling of the week for me back in high school. We started dating when we were sixteen, making future plans. Marriage. Kids. The whole nine yards.

I'd wanted forever with her. Tristan had tried to take her away. And she'd let him.

I remembered that night like it was yesterday.

I showed up at The Pig late, a little drunk from plundering my father's liquor cabinet. I'd heard the rumors about Tristan and Lexie, noticed the signs. We used to be like the three musketeers, all spending time together, but lately, they'd been going off on their own.

Then someone I trusted very much told me they were sleeping together.

I already knew something was wrong. I felt it.

So when I showed up at the Pig and saw them sitting

next to each other, whispering like they had a secret, I just lost it.

I pulled Tristan off the bar stool, hitting him in the jaw as soon as he turned around, his face shocked and pale.

"Oliver, stop it!" Lexie screamed, but I could barely hear her over the blood pounding in my ears. I hit Tristan again, and again, until one of the bouncers pulled me off.

"I know your father, so I'm not going to call the sheriff," Clayton said later, when Tristan was spitting blood into the street and Lexie was comforting him.

My heart was shattered, and I didn't care if they put me in jail or not. But in the end, they let my dad come and get me.

I told Peter the whole story, his eyes wide.

"That sounds wild, man. But at the same time, it's been years. They didn't end up together. Why can't you forgive them?"

"They broke my heart, both of them, together," I muttered. "Yet I went and offered her my cabin to stay in. I can't let her go."

Peter hummed. "Maybe you should tell her that. Maybe it's fate that brought you back together."

I looked at him. "You believe in fate?"

"Kind of," he admitted, smiling sheepishly. "I feel like fate is what brought me and Carlos together."

Carlos was Peter's husband. They'd met in college, went their separate ways, then came back together later in life.

"I don't know if I do," I admitted.

Peter shrugged. "It believes in you," he said cryptically.

I rolled my eyes. "Gross," I said as I chewed my French dip slowly and then popped a fry into my mouth.

He grinned at me. "Romantic. Hopeful. Sweet. Those are the words you should have used."

I rolled my eyes again, but then I said, "So that's your advice? Talk to her?"

"Come clean about your cabin, at least."

"Absolutely not," I said, and Peter snorted out a laugh.

"Whatever you say, boss."

I left the cafe feeling a lot better about things, and that was all that mattered. Peter had served as my friend, not my assistant, and it felt good to get things off my chest.

It was probably for the best that Lexie had left the morning after we hooked up. I didn't want to get wrapped back up in her again. I couldn't for so many reasons, not least of which my child, who didn't deserve to have women coming and going from his life just like his own mother had done.

I thought about the day that he would ask about Suzanne and I grimaced. There were no easy ways to tell a child that his mother had simply dropped him off like the stork on his father's doorstep and then left forever.

"You're bad at women, man," I said to myself. "Really, really bad."

Chapter 9

Lexie

Gillian invited me over for a dinner party on Friday, and all week, I told myself I wasn't going to go. When Friday rolled around, however, I put on my little black dress and a pair of low heels I had borrowed from my sister, and got into Gillian's car.

"You look great," Gillian gushed.

I smiled. "Thank you."

Gillian really was sweet, even if she didn't understand how much she'd been favored for her whole life. She could have grown up to be a real brat but she wasn't. She was kind and gentle-hearted.

I guess maybe I should give her more of a chance to get close to me, but I don't want her to be disappointed when I leave town, which I am planning to do as soon as humanly possible. My first paycheck will need to be devoted to essentials... like clothing, but after that, I'm saving up to just move on with my life.

Her friends were already there, sitting at the table, when we arrived. Gillian must have let them in before coming to pick me up.

I smiled as I introduced myself to everyone. There was Ciara, Gillian's best friend from high school. I'd met her before but hadn't seen her since she was about thirteen. She still looked young, with her curly blonde hair and grey eyes. I also met Ciara's boyfriend, Joshua, who was so shy he could barely look at me when I spoke to him.

Then there was Gray, who Gillian was "kind of dating", at least in her words. He was handsome, tall, and lanky with sandy hair that fell to his shoulders and hazel eyes.

I was the fifth wheel. Great.

"So you're the famous sister she keeps talking about," Gray said, smiling, causing Gillian to blush. I noticed he had a dimple in one cheek.

"That's me," I said. "I'm four years older."

"You don't look it," Joshua piped up, and I smiled brightly at him. He flushed a deep red and looked away, his girlfriend frowning at him.

"You have a crush on her," she accused.

I burst out laughing. "I'm sure no one has a crush on me," I assured her. Although I was a little flattered, Joshua was too young for me, and besides, I didn't make a habit of going after my little sister's friends.

Ciara smiled a little, but I could tell she was peeved, and I made a point to include her in every question I asked Joshua. It worked because he didn't talk much, anyway.

"I heard you were a runaway bride," Gray said, Gillian kicking his shin under the table, making him yelp.

"It's okay," I replied, even though it really wasn't. I was annoyed that Gillian had told her boyfriend my personal history.

"I'm sorry," Gillian whispered, leaning over, and I patted her knee to let her know I wasn't too mad.

"It's quite the story," I said. "Do you guys want to hear about it?"

"Oh, absolutely," Ciara breathed.

I couldn't help but chuckle. "Well, I ran from the church right before the song started announcing the bride was walking down the aisle."

"On foot?" Gray asked, his eyes widening.

"On foot," I admitted. "I hitched a ride with a female trucker, who took me to the airport. I didn't even grab my purse before I ran off, and all I had was a little bit of cash stuffed down my bra. My ex had convinced me to let him handle the finances for a while. It was a bad move."

"That's really brave," Ciara said, and I smiled at her. I wasn't sure how to act around Gilly's friends. I was already starting college by the time she entered high school, therefore, I'd never gotten to know them.

"Thank you," was all I could say.

"Was he a bad guy?" Joshua asked. "Was that the reason you left him?"

I hesitated. "I don't know if he's a bad guy. I just know that he was bad for me. We were bad together."

Ciara nodded. "I've had a couple like that."

Joshua gave her a sharp look. "Who?"

She waved her hand dismissively while Gillian went into the kitchen to open another bottle of wine.

"Gillian is so glad you're back in town," Gray said to me quietly. "She really missed you. Talks about you all the time."

"Really?" It touched my heart that Gillian felt that way about me, especially after all these years. She'd always looked up to me, but because of how our parents were, we'd kind of been pitted against each other.

"Yeah. She doesn't even really talk to your parents anymore because of you," Gray said, and I frowned.

Gillian returned with the bottle and started to fill up our glasses.

"Is that true, Gilly?"

I didn't want to be the reason why Gillian was no longer close to our parents. She'd always been pampered by them; I can't imagine she'd cut them out of her life.

She blinked at me. "What? Gray, are you running your mouth again?"

"Guilty," Gray said with a chuckle.

"Is it true that you're not talking to our parents anymore?" I asked.

"I talk to them," she said defensively. "Just... not that much."

"Because of me?"

Ciara and Josh muttered something to each other, and then Joshua stood up.

"It was really nice to meet you," he said shyly. "But we should go. Ciara has class in the morning."

Ciara nodded. "I'm studying to become a registered nurse."

"Oh, wow," I replied, still thinking about what Gray had said. I was distracted, and I didn't listen much to Ciara as she went on and on about her nursing classes.

After Ciara and Joshua left, Gillian huffed out a breath.

"You should go home," she told Gray. "Lexie and I have plenty to talk about."

Gray sighed, standing up after kissing her temple. "I'm sorry I blabbed."

She huffed out another breath and he pouted. She stood up and kissed him, walking him to the door.

I smiled at them. She really seemed to like him. He was

a little shy for my taste, but perhaps Gillian needed someone like that.

"I'm really sorry about Gray," she said after he left. "I don't know why he can't keep a secret to save his life."

"It's okay," I said, and I meant it. I wasn't angry with her. Besides, everyone had been hanging on to my every word. "Just made me the belle of the ball."

She snorted out a laugh, offering to pour me more wine from the bottle they had left at the table for us. I nodded and she filled my glass before topping off her own.

She sat down across from me. "You know, you're not the only reason I don't talk to Mom and Dad much. It's because... well, it's them."

I nodded solemnly. "I understand. They can be a lot."

"They just kept asking me about you all the time. After a while, that was all our conversations were about."

I blinked. "They did?"

I was shocked to hear that and I couldn't understand why my parents didn't just reach out. It wasn't like they didn't know how to contact me. I'd left my number and address with them before I moved. But they never called. Neither one of them.

"They worry about you, Lex," she said quietly. "I worry about you too."

"I'm fine," I insisted, but was I? It wasn't like I had a career, I was working part time at the local grocery store. I didn't know how I was ever going to get out of Wagontown.

I sniffled quietly, not realizing I was crying until I felt the tears spreading down my cheeks.

Gillian came over to me instantly, putting her arms around me.

"It's going to be okay, sissy. I'll always be here for you."

It was sweet, and it made my heart ache that she was

reaching out when I'd been doing nothing but resenting her. She was a sweet little girl, her whole life, and it was wrong of me to lump her in with our parents.

I buried my face in her shirt and cried for a bit before pulling away with a yawn.

"Stay over tonight," she insisted. "The guest room is always yours."

I shook my head. "Thanks but I think I'd rather go home," I said quietly, and Gillian nodded as if she understood.

A while later, back at home, I laid down on my bed, looking up at the ceiling, and there was only one thing I could think about.

Oliver Stanhope.

The way his hands had felt, roving over my skin. How soft his full mouth was against mine. It'd been so many years since I'd been touched like that, loved like that.

Oliver was always it, and I'd never doubted that. But after everything we'd been through...

It was best to stay away.

Chapter 10

Oliver

I couldn't sleep. It was nearing one in the morning and I didn't know what was wrong with me. Well, actually I did.

Lex was what was wrong with me. I'd almost let myself fall back into her, hook line and sinker.

Stupid.

Before I knew it, I was looking out the window, frowning when I didn't see any lights on at her place. It was so late. Where could she be?

Moments later, I watched as a sleek black car pulled into the driveway and Lex got out, heading into the house. She offered a tired wave at the car as it pulled away.

Who was that? Was she on a date? How'd she meet someone so quickly since arriving back in Wagontown?

My shoulders stiffened as I wondered if it was Tristan. They have some catching up to do and maybe they'd done it tonight. I ran a hand through my hair, frustrated.

I couldn't think about it for too long though because Trent woke up, yelling for me. I rushed into his room, panicked, to find him sitting up in bed, wiping at his eyes and crying.

"Monster," he said in a whispery, hoarse voice. "The monsters were trying to get me. They got you, Daddy," he whimpered, and I picked him up, humming to him lightly.

"It's okay, Trent. Monsters aren't real, remember?" I soothed, patting his back, but he pulled away, frowning at me.

"They tried to eat my toes, Dad," he said solemnly, and I had to bite back laughter.

"I'm so sorry, honey. Do you want to get a snack or have some tea?"

"Both."

I carried him into the kitchen, sitting him down in his booster seat while I made a pot of peppermint tea, his favorite, and a couple of peanut butter and jelly sandwiches.

Trent often had nightmares and I worried about that a lot. Was it because his mom wasn't around? Was I doing the right thing, distracting him, and not making him go back to bed immediately? This whole parenting thing didn't come with a manual.

Trent sniffled slightly before digging into his peanut butter and jelly and sipping his tea. I smiled at him, ruffling his hair.

"Feeling better, buddy?"

"A little," he said in a tired, raspy voice. He looked up at me with wide eyes. "Do you think the monsters want my toes because they're clean and smell good? Because I could stop washing them."

I couldn't help but snicker and he frowned at me.

"I think they like dirty toes even more," I replied with a serious expression, and Trent's eyes widened. I laughed.

"I'm only joking, buddy. There's no such thing as monsters."

"Then why do they come in my dreams?" he asked, huffing out a breath in frustration.

"Dreams come from your mind, Trent. Something deep down that you're afraid of," I tried to explain as I sipped my tea.

"What are you afraid of, Daddy?"

He tilted his head as he looked up at me. I opened my mouth but didn't know how to answer.

"I guess I'm mostly afraid of being a bad dad," I said quietly.

Trent climbed off his booster seat and into my lap, hugging me tightly. "You're the best dad in the world."

My heart swelled and I hugged him back just as tight. "I love you, Trent. You ready to go back to bed?" I asked after a brief pause.

He shook his head fiercely. "I think you know what I need," he said promptly, and I couldn't help but smile.

"Rock and roll?" I asked, and Trent grinned, nodding his head in agreement.

I chuckled and stood up, taking his small hand, and leading him to the back of the house and onto the terrace near the pool.

I turned on the boombox as loud as I could stand it. He started to dance, moving and grooving, but soon his dancing became slow, and within a couple of songs, he climbed up into my lap and fell asleep, snoring lightly against my chest.

I rubbed his back, knowing he would probably wake up if I took him back into the house right away. So I sat there and listened to the music for a while, classic rock, Trent's favorite, and thought about better days.

Everything was perfect when I was eighteen. I had a

sweet girl and the world at my feet. I had my best friend, Tristan, who was there for me through thick and thin, and my parents were happily married.

One day, Lex wore a yellow sundress to my house. I pinned her against my bedroom wall, arms above her head, our fingers intertwined, until she was panting against my neck.

When she pulled away, laughing, I kissed the freckles across her nose.

That good memory led to something bad, and I knew it, so I tried to push it out of my mind.

As I stared across the grounds down to the cabin where Lex was, a small figure came into view, stalking across the grass.

I frowned, squinting, and standing up, jostling Trent in my arms. He didn't stir.

I knew it was Lex before she came into focus. It was like something inside me always knew when she was near, and that was rather inconvenient given how she'd broken my heart and put it in a blender.

How do you just stop loving someone no matter what they did to you?

Lexie made it up the hill, glaring at me, but her face softened when she saw the little bundle in my arms.

"Ollie," she breathed. "You've got a little one."

I couldn't help but smile. "That I do," I admitted, walking over to the boombox and turning down the music. "I assume the noise is why you came hauling ass up here."

Lexie snorted out a laugh and it wrinkled her nose in the cutest way. "I thought you were having a party."

"This late?" I asked incredulously. "Please, Lex, we're old now."

"Speak for yourself, mister." She swayed toward me and Trent. "He's really yours?"

"Nah, I just took him in. Like a stray." Her eyes widened and I laughed. "Yes, Lex, he's mine."

"How old is he?"

"Five," I say, brushing Trent's hair back from his face. "Listen, I've got to take him inside but... stay for a beer, why don't you?"

Lexie looked at me a bit warily, but then shrugged and sat down in the patio chair across from mine.

I took Trent into the house and upstairs to his room, tucking him in and humming to him, hoping he wouldn't wake up again. He didn't, thankfully.

My heart thudded in my chest. Why had I asked her to stay? What was I thinking? I've been desperately trying to get her out of my head yet I just invited her to have a beer?

Despite my contradictory thoughts, I grabbed two bottles from the fridge and popped them open before walking back out onto the patio.

She sat cross-legged in the patio chair, wearing a pair of sweats and a baggy t-shirt. She didn't appear to have any makeup on, and her hair was piled messily up on top of her head. She looked unexpectedly sexy, and I had to catch my breath.

I wanted to ask her where she'd been tonight. I wanted to ask her who she'd been with.

But that was none of my business. Not anymore.

Instead, I cleared my throat. "I guess you probably have a lot of questions."

She shrugged. "I guess it's really none of my business."

She was right, it wasn't, but I was still surprised she didn't ask. Maybe I was just assuming she still cared when she honestly didn't.

She looked up at me. "I'm more surprised that you're here at all. Are you stalking me or something?"

I scoffed, anger rushing through me. "No, of course not. If it wasn't for me, you'd have had nowhere to go."

"I have somewhere to go," she mumbled. I noticed there was no fire in her eyes. Seeing that made me deflate, made my shoulders slump.

Without fire, there was no love. And maybe there never had been, at least not for her. Me, on the other hand, I had fallen so deep in love that it felt like I was dying every time I had to be away from her, even if it was only for a few days.

It had become clear that she didn't feel the same way. Not then, not now.

I took in a deep breath. "Well, I'm sorry about the music. It's the only way he'll go back to sleep."

"You were married?" she asked quietly, and there it was, some hint that she was at least a little bit interested in what I had been up to. I hated the way it made my heart soar.

I shook my head. "No, it was nothing. We only saw each other a handful of times. But when Trent came along, she realized she just wasn't ready to be a mother. Dropped him off on my doorstep when he was a few weeks old."

"Holy cow," Lexie said, her eyes widening. "She literally just left him? You haven't heard from her?"

I shook my head. "I filed paperwork with the court, and she signed over her rights. She assumed that I'd be a better parent, I guess."

"And you're not angry?" She looked at me incredulously, her head tilted.

"I was, for a while. But Trent is the best thing that's ever happened to me. He changed my life."

Her wide eyes softened. "I always thought you'd be a really good dad."

Hearing that stung, hitting me right in the chest with emotion, and I tore my eyes away from hers.

"Are you still angry that I live here?"

She sighed. "A little. I didn't want charity. Not from Gillian and not from you."

"It's not charity," I said quietly, looking into her eyes. "The place is just sitting there, empty. Besides, you'll pay what you can in rent eventually. That's more than what I was getting before."

She glanced up at me, biting her lip, and God, how I wanted to thumb it from between her teeth and kiss her.

"Okay," she said quietly. "I'm sorry I interrupted your time with your son."

"You didn't," I said quickly, though I didn't know why I said it. Why did I want her to stay so badly? Why couldn't I just let her go? "Stay for another beer. We're neighbor's now, right?"

A smile broke across her pretty face, and she tipped her half-empty beer toward me.

"I suppose we are."

My breath caught in my throat, and I sat down heavily on the patio chair across from her.

She drained the rest of her beer and stood, walking past me to throw it in the big trash can by the house.

What I did next was the stupidest thing I'd done in years. Again.

I grabbed her around the wrist, pulled her onto my lap, and then I kissed her.

Chapter 11

Lexie

All the oxygen seemed to go out of the air when Oliver kissed me, but wasn't that how it always worked? There was never anyone on the planet but him whenever he kissed me. Tonight, I was surrounded by the taste of beer and his sandalwood cologne. It touched deep places in my heart and my soul.

I moaned into his mouth and turned to face him before cupping his cheeks and kissing him again while straddling his hips on the small chair, which creaked beneath us. I was relieved it was sturdy enough to hold both of us.

Oliver breathed out something against my lips and I pulled away, frowning.

"What?" I asked.

He shook his head and tried to kiss me again. I pressed a finger to his lips and shook my head. "Tell me what you said."

He looked at me for a moment, then a lopsided smile spread over his face. "I missed you," he admitted.

I continued to frown at him. "You aren't supposed to do that anymore," I replied.

He laughed, and the sound warmed my heart in spite of my desire to keep some distance between us. "I know that," he told me. "But I missed you anyway."

I almost told him how I missed him too, every day, all the time, even when I was engaged to Dick. But that wouldn't be helpful for either of us, not really, not when I was trying to create some space between us so I could escape this little town once and for all.

His arms went around my waist, pulling me back in as he pressed his forehead against mine.

"How come you never had kids?" he asked, and I blinked in shock that he wanted to talk while our bodies were pressed up against each other like this.

I swallowed hard. "I don't know."

Oliver pulled away just enough to look into my eyes, confusion on his face.

"Yeah, you do. Marriage and kids were all we talked about while we were together. You were so excited to be a mama someday."

I licked my lips. "He wasn't the right guy."

"Why not?" Oliver asked, and from the way he was looking at me, I figured he wasn't going to let that slide.

"I don't even know if he was a good guy," I whispered. "Things changed after we got engaged. He used to be so sweet, bringing me flowers, texting me every day, writing me poetry."

Oliver rolled his eyes, but I ignored it, continuing.

"But then after we moved in together, when things got more serious, he became different."

"Bad different?"

I nodded. "Controlling, different. I could be at the corner store and if I was gone longer than he thought I should be, he'd call me, over and over. Eventually he'd just show up, angry."

I remembered a time when Dick had caused a scene in front of the owner of the store, and it had been so embarrassing. I didn't tell that to Oliver, though, because his face was already red, and he looked like he might explode.

"I wish I was going to have the chance to meet him," he said in a low tone.

I raised an eyebrow, smiling. "Why?"

"So that I could kill him."

I couldn't help but bark out a laugh at that. "Well, he's gone now. The way I ran off, I doubt he'll ever want to speak to me again."

"You'd be surprised," Oliver muttered. "You're a rare find, Lex."

"Am I?" I asked in a cooing voice, my fingers playing at the hair at the nape of his neck. I couldn't help myself. It was just like old times on his father's back porch and I knew it was dangerous. I was so close to falling right back in love with him.

Maybe I would have pulled away if Oliver hadn't leaned up and kissed me deeply at that moment.

I moaned into his mouth and my hips rolled against him, feeling his erection through the fabric of his sweats.

Just talking about Dick had made me feel dirty and sad all over again. I wanted to erase that, make myself feel powerful and beautiful, and Oliver had always made me feel those things and so much more.

Why didn't we just talk through our issues back then? my brain whispered. What's stopping you from doing so now?

I really didn't want to be thinking about logistics with Oliver's hardness pressing into my thigh and his lips pressed to the pulse in my throat, so I shoved away the meanderings of my distracted brain. There would be time enough for regrets later. Right now, I wanted to feel happy again, and Oliver was offering me everything I needed to accomplish that goal.

Oliver growled, grabbing the back of my head to kiss me harder, and then he stood up, carrying me with him over to the side of his house, pressing me against it. His lips moved down my neck, and everything felt like it was on fire, my skin burning, my heart beating too fast.

"Remember this?" he whispered in between kisses. "We used to hide around corners and in closets just to make out. We were crazy for one another."

"I remember," I said back, and boy did I ever. So many different memories of stolen moments with Oliver had been coming back to me lately. We had just been kids, but we had been crazy for one another, and we had taken every chance we could to kiss, fondle, and enjoy each other.

*Don't let this go any further. Stop it now, t*he voice in the back of my head warned me, but I didn't listen. I didn't want to listen. I wanted Oliver. I had always wanted Oliver.

He carried me inside and up the stairs, stopping along the way to kiss me and touch me, and by the time he laid me down on his bed, I was panting with lust.

Oliver tore off his shirt with one hand, shoving down his sweats to free himself with the other, and my mouth watered at the sight of him. His erection stood thick and proud against his hard, toned stomach.

I started to scramble out of my clothes, Oliver helping me. When my tank top went over my head, he put his mouth on my nipple and my back arched.

"Oliver," I managed. "I want you so badly."

"Not nearly as badly as I want you," he muttered

against my neck, then pulled my shorts off, tossing them onto the floor and spreading my thighs with his knee.

It looked like it was going to be rough and quick, and I couldn't say I minded. Not one bit.

"I was going to do something romantic, but..." he muttered as he tumbled me back onto the mountain of pillows resting against the headboard.

"Shut up and fuck me," I said.

He glanced up at me sharply, his brown eyes reflecting his surprise. I giggled and shrugged.

"I'm a big girl now," I assured him. "I'm not afraid to ask for what I want."

A smile tucked itself into the corner of his mouth and he leaned closer to me, his lips just barely touching mine. His longish hair tickled my nose where it fell over his forehead.

"And what do you want?" he said quietly. I felt the words as much as heard them.

"You," I whispered, being fully honest for a moment. I left out all the other baggage that went with that single word. We both knew the truth, even if we denied it in the light of day, but here, in the dark, with our skin pressed together, we could be honest with one another.

"In that case," he said back, before kissing me slowly, his tongue tangling with mine. Oliver pressed into me, and my eyes rolled into the back of my head as pleasure rocketed through my core.

"God, you feel so good," Oliver groaned, dropping down on his forearms to kiss me as he started to move his hips.

The way he dragged against my sweet spot caused me to get close to the edge quickly, and I whined when he slowed his strokes.

"Lex," he whispered, looking into my eyes. "This is where you're supposed to be."

My breath caught in my throat. "You can't stay things like that, Ollie. Not now. It's not fair."

I thought, for a brief, terrible moment, that he would pull out of me, leave me there wanting, but he didn't. He just tucked his head into my neck and moved his hips faster, grunting.

I wrapped my legs around his narrow waist, fighting back memories of the backseat of his truck, the meadow down by the river with the moon shining over us, the time that we had had sex under a blanket in the basement of my house, giggling and trying unsuccessfully to be silent.

"God, Lexie," he said, slamming home inside of me, his voice muffled by my hair, his lips touching my shoulder.

I reached up to stroke my hands along his skin, enjoying the feeling of his muscles clenching in his bowed back, admiring the power that I had over him in this situation, loving that I could affect him so strongly.

"Come for me," he murmured against my skin, and as if my body had been waiting for his command, I shattered, biting his shoulder to stifle my cries of pleasure. The last thing we needed was his child wandering in and asking who was in bed with his dad.

I clung to Oliver as my orgasm rolled over me, and he groaned and followed me over the edge, spilling inside of me, hot and warm.

When he pulled out of me, I felt empty, hollow, and I swallowed hard. "I'm sorry," I said quickly. "I'll go."

He collapsed next to me, wrapping his arm tight around my waist. "Don't you dare," he said in a low tone. "You did that to me last time, and it drove me crazy."

"Why?" I asked in a hoarse whisper, and he stroked my face.

"I don't know," he finally said, looking away from me. "I guess I just thought we had more history than that."

"You can't miss me," I said to him sternly, hoping to convince my own traitorous heart that it also couldn't keep missing him.

He smiled slightly and pulled me into his arms, nuzzling against my neck. It felt like I was back home in his bed, everything about being around him did. It was as if no time had passed at all, and my heart didn't know the difference, opening like a flower while he held me.

He kissed me again, and I let myself love him, just for that moment. It wouldn't be forever. Right? I could allow myself this one, selfish moment because I needed it, needed him.

I woke up a few hours later, daylight streaming through the windows. I glanced over at Oliver and my heart ached.

I thought about the great life he had, his beautiful son, everything he'd made for himself. I didn't have that. I didn't have any of that. I'd left it all behind.

I had to admit to myself that I was a little jealous of his life, and not just because I wanted it for my own. I wanted it *with* Oliver. That was always the plan growing up. I'd get settled in a career, and I'd have Oliver and everything else I'd ever wanted.

But that wasn't what happened. Instead, we'd gotten into a senseless fight that ended everything.

My chest hurt as my heart started to race again, this time from panic and fear of falling back in love with him.

I had to get out of there. Besides, I shouldn't be around when his son woke up. That would be awkward and confusing for him.

I stood up, slowly extricating myself from Oliver's arms so he wouldn't wake, then made my way to the top of the stairs.

I hadn't gotten a good look at the house last night, but today, I could see how homey it was. It had Oliver's touch, but it felt like a home instead of just a bachelor pad.

The furniture looked comfortable, and the décor was simple but tasteful. Although it lacked a woman's touch, I believed it was a very happy home, and for some reason, that made my eyes well with tears.

I hurried out of the house, all but sprinting across the terrace and grounds to get to my place.

I was breathing hard by the time I got to the cabin, but I managed to get inside and make a pot of coffee before a knock sounded at my door.

Frowning, certain of who it could be, I walked to the door and looked through the peephole.

As expected, Oliver stood there. And he looked mad.

I opened the door and took in a deep breath as he stormed in.

"You always run away," he accused.

I stood there for a moment, staring at him, anger rushing through my veins. "You dumped me, remember?" I said shakily, clenching my fists at my sides. "You're the one who broke up with me, all those years ago."

"What else was I supposed to do?" he shot back.

"You were supposed to trust me," I whispered.

Chapter 12

Oliver

I was suddenly jolted back into the past at Lexie's words, and it washed over me like a tidal wave.

My father had told me something unthinkable. I didn't believe it, not for a minute, but I had to talk to her all the same.

I needed to see her. I wanted to prove my father wrong. I knew he hadn't ever liked Lexie, but he wouldn't lie to me about her and my best friend.

But I saw them, sitting together at the bar, laughing. I saw red. I barely knew what I was doing. I felt myself hitting Tristan, but I didn't know I was going to do it. Everything felt like a bad dream, a nightmare.

I looked up at Lexie, my eyes wide and wet.

"Tristan? It had to be Tristan?"

"What the hell are you talking about, Oliver?" Lexie hissed, pulling at my arm, sniffling out a sob.

"You're sleeping with my best friend!" I yelled, wrenching away from her, and standing up to face her,

ignoring Tristan even though part of me wanted to strangle him.

This wasn't really about Tristan. This was about me and Lex, and what we had. What we used to have.

"Oliver, what are you..." she started, but I couldn't listen to any more of her lies.

I had stalked away, and that was the last time I'd spoken to either of them until recently.

I blinked away the memories to find Lex looking up at me with wide green eyes.

"My dad told me about you two," I told her, trying not to feel the old resentment. I felt sick, just like I had that day.

She scowled. "Why did your dad dislike me so much?" she muttered. Her eyes locked onto mine again. "Also, you knew he didn't like me. Would it have been so hard to imagine that he might not have had your best intentions in mind when he told you that?"

"It's water under the bridge," I finally said, pushing all of the thoughts, memories, and heartaches away. "I forgive you."

"That's the thing, Oliver. It's not. You're still angry, you still haven't apologized... to me or to Tristan. It's not water under any bridge because you aren't over it," she scoffed, and of course, she was right, but I didn't want to talk about this any more.

God help me, despite everything, I wanted her back in my life. I needed her around, needed her near me, and last night only proved that. Waking up this morning without her, thinking she might have run away again... I couldn't handle that.

I needed her.

"Why did you leave this morning?"

"I didn't want your kid to find me in the house," she muttered.

I nodded. "Fair enough."

"I also need to look for jobs," she said.

"You have a job," I insisted.

"Yes, and I'm grateful for it," she said, then paused with a sigh. "It's part time, Oliver, and I'll never make enough money to get out of Wagontown if I don't get a second job."

"You're going to leave Wagontown again?"

She stared at me incredulously. "Of course I am, Oliver. It's not like this place is full of great memories for me. I just want to get the hell out of here. Also, there's no way for me to make a living here, if you haven't noticed. I can't even pay you rent. "

My heart sank. She was going to leave me all over again, and I didn't know how I was going to handle it.

I assumed not well.

"You always wanted to get out of Wagontown," I muttered.

"We never would have made it together anyway," she said in a soft voice, and my head was spinning.

How could she say that? I had planned to marry her, have a family with her. Even now, I still wanted her, though I didn't know in what capacity that was possible.

In the meantime, however, if I could get her a job and keep her near me...

"Why don't you work for me?" I suggested. Lexie looked at me, blinking.

"Work for you? Like as an assistant or something?"

I chuckled. "Nothing like that." I already had an excellent assistant. "I'm buying a bar, and you could work there."

"Oh, Richy-rich," she teased, a smile on her face. "Must be nice to be able to just buy a bar."

I shrugged. "So will you do it?" I asked her.

"What, work as a bartender?"

"It's a living," I argued, and she took in a breath.

"You're right. I'm not going to turn up my nose at it. I'll take the job."

She stuck out her hand for me to shake, and I shook it, smiling.

Things seemed to be looking up.

"Promise me one thing," I said, leaning down to her ear.

"Yes?" she asked, looking up into my eyes.

"No more running," I said firmly. "When you're ready to leave, talk to me first. Let me know you're going."

She was quiet for a long moment, but then finally nodded.

"All right. No more running."

I nodded back, slowly moving toward the door, hoping against hope she'd stop me, kiss me, but she didn't. She just looked away and started making herself coffee.

"I'll get you some more information about the job at the bar," I said awkwardly.

She nodded, barely glancing at me. "Cool."

Cool? I sighed. We were back to square one on the intimacy front. I hated that, but there wasn't anything I could do about it right now.

As I walked back up the hill to my place, I thought about how I was already in too deep.

I needed to back off, not continue jumping in.

But instead, I found myself pulling out my phone, calling Clayton. We'd been in talks about the Pig for a while, but I'd never had a reason to pull the trigger.

Until now.

"Hello?" Theresa, his wife, answered.

"It's Oliver Stanhope," I said quietly into the phone,

letting myself out the back door. "I was hoping that we could meet up today. Finally sign the papers."

I could feel her hesitation through the line. "I don't know, Oliver. We've received another offer—"

"I'll double it," I said firmly, hearing a surprised gasp on the other end of the line.

"Double it? You don't even know what it is!"

"Doesn't matter. You know I can cover it."

"All right. Come on over then, I'll get everything printed out."

"Be there in an hour."

I hung up the phone, then hurried upstairs to dress simply in a button-up shirt and a pair of black jeans. I didn't need a three-piece suit to close on the purchase of a dive bar, and besides, Clayton's wife, Theresa, and I knew each other. She knew my family and had been friends with my mother.

When I arrived at the Pig, she met me at the door.

"How's your mom?" she asked quietly, and I took in a deep breath. I knew that Theresa must know what a hard time my parents were having, how they'd split up recently. They hadn't mentioned the word "divorce" yet, but it seemed to hang heavy in the air every time I was around them. I couldn't get them in the same room together, not anymore.

"She's hanging in there," I muttered, not wanting to speak much on that subject. Thankfully, Theresa seemed to understand, simply nodding before sliding a file folder across the bar to me.

"Can I get you a beer?"

"Any kind of ale, please," I replied. She poured me a pint that I barely sipped while looking over the contract.

It seemed straightforward, but I knew my lawyer,

Andrew Taylor, would want to have a look at it before I signed anything. I also knew he'd try to talk me out of it. He kept saying that bars were money pits, but I begged to differ. I'd seen the markup on shots of liquor and wholesale prices, and I thought it would be a great secondary income.

Besides, if it didn't work out, I was only out a couple million. I had plenty more in various bonds, properties, and in my bank account. I'd done well for myself, so why shouldn't I indulge this little bar-owning fantasy?

I asked Theresa to email me the contract so I could forward it to my attorney.

"Clayton is okay with this?"

"As long as you go by his rules and don't fire any of his staff."

"Of course."

She shrugged. "Then he's good to go."

"Where is he, anyway?"

Theresa grinned. "He should be packing."

"Packing?"

"We're going to the Bahamas."

I couldn't help but grin. If anyone deserved it, it was them.

Once I received notification from Andrew that the contract was legit and good to sign, I called a mobile notary, and by the time lunch rolled around, I was the proud owner of The Pig in the Poke.

Theresa shook my hand.

"Say hello to your mother for me."

I nodded, knowing I'd do exactly that. I'd talked to Mom about buying the bar, and she thought it would be a good investment. Besides, I hadn't seen her at all since Lex came back into my life. She knew what happened all those years ago. She'd understand.

Trent was with her so I might as well pick him up. This was all the work I was going to do today anyway; everything else would be handled by my assistant and the board. It was nice to be able to make my own hours, although I usually worked too much for comfort.

Maybe that could change now that I had the bar. I could work there, instead, spend some time away from the business I'd worked so hard to build. It could help me avoid burnout, for sure.

I didn't buy a bar just to employ Lexie. Did I?

* * *

When I arrived at Mom's, I expected Trent to come running out when he saw my car pull up, but he didn't. Mom came to the door, smiling.

"He's in the backyard with the neighbor boy. They're skipping rocks out at the creek."

I smiled. That sounded like exactly what I wanted Trent to be doing all summer. I wanted him to make friends, branch out, stop being so attached to me. It wasn't that I didn't love his sweetness and snuggles, but I didn't want him to be lonely when school started back up.

He'd had a hard time adjusting to preschool, and I worried that kindergarten would be even worse.

"How old is the neighbor boy?" I asked, and Mom shrugged.

"Six, seven. He's about the same size as Trent, though."

"He's a big kid."

"Just like you always were," she said, beaming at me. She looked tired.

"Mom, can we talk?" I asked quietly. She raised an eyebrow, her brown eyes widening.

"Of course, Oliver. Anytime."

"I'll make us some coffee," I suggested.

"Decaf for me," she pointed out, putting a hand to her heart. I winced. It reminded me that she had been diagnosed with an arrhythmia that could prove dangerous. My parents were both getting up there in years, and it was scary, all the health issues that had popped up lately.

I made us each a cup of instant, decaf for her, and sat down at the table across from her.

"Something on your mind, son?" she asked, her eyes wrinkling around the corners as she gave me a small frown.

I sighed. "A lot of things, really." I paused. "I went ahead and bought that tavern downtown."

"Tess' place? Oh, that's wonderful," she gushed. Tess was Theresa's nickname. "Your father and I...." she trailed off.

I cleared my throat, not sure if I should push.

"Go on."

"Your father and I had our first dance there," she said softly.

"Mom, why don't you talk to him? I know he'd love to hear from you," I suggested gently.

Her face hardened. "We're not here to talk about me and your dad. We're here to talk about you. What's going on, Ollie?"

She was right. I was deflecting. There was a lot on my mind.

"Lex is back in town."

"I know you don't mean Alexandra Tripp," she said flatly.

"That's exactly who I mean," I said, rubbing a hand across my face. "She's staying in my cabin."

My mother looked at me curiously, tilting her head. "How do you feel about that?"

"I..." I paused, trying to find the words. "I don't know."

She hummed in the back of her throat, sipping her coffee. "Why is she staying at your cabin? Doesn't she have family? Her sister still lives in town, from what I remember."

"They don't exactly get along," I mumbled. I wasn't quite sure what was going on between Lex and Gillian, but I knew that Lexie didn't want to be a burden to her.

"And it's your responsibility to take care of her? After everything?" Mom's voice was only a little icy. She knew the full story, but she had always loved Lex, always wanted the best for her. Even though she'd hurt me, I didn't think my mother hated her.

"It's not my responsibility, but it's... it's been years. It's over. Water under the bridge."

"Is that how you really feel, Ollie?"

"Yes," I said quickly, knowing it was a lie, guilt burning hot at the back of my mind.

She smiled. "Well, you've always been a good guy. I know you'll do the right thing."

The right thing.

What was that, exactly?

"What if I don't know what that is, Mom?"

She spread her hands out. "None of us ever really do," she said. "Most of the time, everything in life is an educated guess."

I smiled at her. "Rolling the dice over and over, I guess."

She nodded. "Sometimes you get lucky, is the thing," she said with a wink.

"Sometimes you don't," I said in a sober tone of voice.

"But it's the risk that makes it all worth it," she replied with a knowing look, patting my hand.

I smiled at her. Everything with Lexie always felt high-stakes, exciting, worth doing. Maybe that was why I just couldn't let her go, even though I had truly wanted to a time or two.

It was just that so much of my life was predictable, easy, reliable. Even parenting wasn't usually all that exciting because my kid was easy to take care of. I realized abruptly that Lexie gave things life, and color, and made stuff fun for me. I hadn't experienced much of that since she left.

How had I missed that before?

My head was all over the place as I drove Trent home and put him to bed. I couldn't stop thinking about her. Even right up to when I closed my eyes that night to go to sleep, I was thinking about Lexie.

I wanted her to stay in Wagontown. For good.

What that meant for me, I didn't know.

Chapter 13

Lexie

A couple of weeks had passed since I'd last seen Oliver or his little boy. It was mostly because it was tourist season in Wagontown, and the grocery store had me running around in circles. I had plenty of hours right now at work, but that would die down as summer waned into spring, and by then, I was hoping to have Oliver's bartending job as a means of income.

God knew my little paycheck at the grocery store wasn't going to get me out of this godforsaken town. With my first check, I purchased myself a cell phone. The only numbers I had in it were Oliver's, his grandmother's, and Gillian's. I found myself grateful that I didn't have Dick's number memorized, and that he didn't have this new number.

I texted Gillian with my new number, and she immediately called me. I couldn't help but smile at the exuberance in her voice.

"We have to celebrate!"

"Celebrate a new phone?" I asked with a chuckle, but she didn't join in.

"You're moving up in the world, Lex. You've got that

cabin, you got a job, and now you've got a new phone. We should celebrate your newfound independence."

Although I hadn't exactly told her about how controlling Dick was, I felt that Gillian got the idea, knowing how he'd isolated me from my family and friends.

She seemed to want to make a big deal about me getting away, and why shouldn't I let her? I didn't have a shift at the grocery store for two more days, and Oliver hadn't approached me about starting at the bar just yet. I assumed he was still getting things together, maybe even remodeling. It could be weeks.

"All right," I agreed. "Let's celebrate."

"Just you and me. We'll go out."

"Where?"

"The Pig, of course," she said, as if there wasn't half a dozen other bars in Wagontown.

I couldn't complain. After all, I'd frequented the Pig when I was younger, and it still held a lot of nostalgia for me.

"Let's eat first," I suggested. "I'm starving."

"Bonnie's it is!" Gillian cheered.

Bonnie's was a local wing place where they had all kinds of crazy flavors and Gillian had loved it since we were kids.

I couldn't help but smile at her excitement. We chatted for a moment longer before I hung up to get dressed.

I decided on a simple milkmaid sundress, even though I didn't have a ton of cleavage to fill it out. I loved the shape of it though, and I figured my toned legs would make up for the lack of cleavage.

It wasn't like I was dressing to impress, exactly, but it'd been a while since I'd been out, and I wanted to look nice.

You're healing, a voice whispered in my head. I

wouldn't admit to myself that the reason so much of my confidence had come back was Oliver's admiration. Dick had made me feel average, normal, boring, unremarkable. Oliver made me feel desirable, special, unique, and sexy.

I looked at myself in the mirror. I looked really pretty. I realized I hadn't thought that in years and tears pricked my eyes. How had I let that jerk make me feel so small, so unloved?

I didn't want to go down the road of linking his bad treatment with the way that my folks had always minimized me. Today was a day to be happy. I was the owner of a new cell phone after all.

I shoved the bad thoughts and memories away, grinned at myself in the mirror, and started working on my hair and makeup.

I curled my hair so that it flowed down my back and put on a bit of smoky makeup. By the time I was done, I was happy with what I saw in the mirror. It was probably the first time in a long time I felt good about myself, and I had to admit that was partially because of Oliver.

He still wanted me. After all this time.

I took in a deep breath. I couldn't believe that I'd accepted a job offer from him, especially since I found out I was living on his property, but it was the only opportunity I had to get out of this town and back to my life.

Being in Wagontown was like being in a nostalgic bubble, as if my real life was somewhere else, and I was living in some kind of fantasy. In the fantasy, I hadn't been damaged by years of poor treatment by those who professed to love me. I was just Lexie, who loved football games, drinking beer with friends, and... sharing kisses and maybe a bit more with her boyfriend in the corner of the bar.

It was all a fantasy, it couldn't be real, but I was

enjoying leaning into the good times from the past, being the person I used to be.

The fantasy in my head was a dream where Oliver could be mine. Where we could have a family.

Gillian knocked on my door, startling me from my thoughts. I jumped and headed quickly to the peephole. I didn't know why I was so nervous. It wasn't like Dick had any idea where I was. Yet I kept expecting him to show up.

Gillian frowned as she walked inside, dressed in a pink pastel dress with a matching bag, always stylish. It fit her petite frame well.

"What's wrong with you? You look like you've seen a ghost."

I shook my head. "Nothing. You ready to go?"

She grinned. "I'm always ready for Bonnie's Caribbean jerk wings," she said, licking her lips.

I smiled wanly and got into her car, a weird feeling at the back of my neck. Why was I so afraid Dick would show up? He'd never hurt me, at least not physically.

But his tongue could just be so damn sharp....

"You're far away today," Gillian accused.

"Thinking about my ex," I admitted.

She paused, surprise evident on her face. "You don't talk much about him. Don't talk much about anything to do with your life recently, actually."

"I'm sorry," I said quietly, and I meant it. I reached over to take her hand and she squeezed it. Maybe I'd been wrong all these years to avoid her. She was my baby sister, after all. We should have a closer relationship.

Gillian gave me a smile. "No worries, sis. We've got all the time in the world."

I went quiet, not wanting to say I was on the next flight out of here as soon as possible.

Bonnie's was packed for lunch, and we had to wait about fifteen minutes for a table near the window, but Gillian didn't seem to mind.

She chatted about her friends, her job, everything, while I just nodded and smiled in the right places. She'd always been a talker.

At the table, she ordered her usual and I bit my lip, looking at the flavors on the menu. There was so much to choose from.

"Try the Thai curry," a voice said behind me, making me jump. "It's to die for."

I turned slightly to see Oliver, smiling, standing in the to-go line near our table.

Licking my lips, I nodded at the server to let her know that would be my order.

"Picking up lunch for me and the kiddo," Oliver said easily, as if we were friends, as if he wasn't inside me just a couple of weeks ago.

I cleared my throat. "He looks too young for wings."

"He loves the boneless buffalo," he said with a chuckle. "Kid loves spice, I don't get it."

I smiled, thinking of the sleeping boy he'd been carrying a few nights ago at his house. I would have known that the little boy was his, even at a glance. He looked just like the pictures I had seen of Oliver when he was a kid.

The thought of little Olivers running around, calling me mommy, made my heart squeeze in my chest. I had fully expected for that to be my future for so long. I had imagined how our kids would look as they grew, had picked out their names and everything.

I didn't want to examine how much it had hurt to see Oliver cradling a child and carrying him to bed when I knew that the future I had always imagined would never come to pass.

"See you later?" Oliver said hopefully as he got his food, and I nodded briefly as Gillian just stared at the two of us, mouth wide open.

"You have *got* to spill what's going on there," she whispered as soon as the door closed behind him.

"There's nothing to tell," I muttered, knowing that was a lie. There was plenty to tell, but I didn't know where to even start.

"You were crazy about him in high school," Gillian pointed out. "I remember that much."

"That was a long time ago," I mumbled, picking at my napkin, and tearing it into little pieces.

Gillian narrowed her eyes. "You know, I was so happy when you came back to town. I thought maybe I could finally have my sister be my best friend. But you're just so stiff and closed off, Lex."

"I'm sorry," I said again, looking up at her with a small smile. "I'll try to be better." I took in a deep breath. "Oliver offered me a job."

"A job?" she asked incredulously. "That's all?"

"That's not all," I said quietly. "We've been... well, we've been hooking up, I guess you'd call it."

She gasped. "My sister, the tramp."

"Stop," I said, laughing, knowing she was teasing. "It's not like that. We're both adults, right? Haven't you ever had a fling? Also, that's a heck of a thing to say to me after shaming me into being more open with you."

She chuckled. "Sorry. I couldn't resist teasing you. But, no, I would never even want to get involved with my high school sweetheart. That just makes things complicated."

"It sure does," I agreed, thankful when the wings

arrived. Gillian dug in. She couldn't ask questions with her mouth full.

The Thai curry wings were, in fact, to die for. They were delicious paired with the house blue cheese dip, and I had sauce all over my face within minutes.

But that was par for the course at Bonnie's.

I wiped off my face with the wet naps they provided, and Gillian grinned at me.

"This was nice," she said. "How about instead of going to the Pig tonight we stay in with some ice cream and wine? You can tell me all about Oliver." She paused. "And your ex-almost-husband."

I thought about it for a long moment. "You know what, that sounds amazing."

We headed back to Gillian's place. Once we got inside, she threw me a pair of sweats and a t-shirt to put on. We sat on the couch watching bad reality television while each eating a pint of ice cream. Mint chocolate for Gillian, and Rocky Road for me.

There was something so sweet about it, something so comforting. We should have been like this years ago. It was my fault we weren't. I was going to make up for it, though. I was going to be the big sister I always should have been.

No reason why we couldn't start now.

I leaned against her. "So tell me about this guy you're dating."

Gillian blushed. "Gray? You met him."

"Briefly. I don't know the backstory though."

"It's boring," she huffed, but I kept looking at her curiously. She took in a deep breath. "Okay, so we met at work."

"Is he your superior? Is this going to sound like a romcom movie?" I teased.

She snorted. "No, we're both lowly office workers. I asked him out, and, well, it's been off and on ever since."

I raised an eyebrow. "What do you mean by off and on?"

Gillian sighed. "I don't know. He doesn't seem to want a relationship," she said glumly.

I frowned. "I don't know if you should be dating guys like that, Gilly."

"I know, I know," she groaned, "but he's so sweet and he treats me well when we're together." She shoved a big spoonful of mint chocolate chip into her mouth.

"When you're together?" I kept asking questions because I wanted to know more about him, wanted to protect her.

"Yeah. For instance, he doesn't text a lot when we're apart. I'm always the first to text him then I don't hear back right away, that kind of thing," she admitted.

I frowned deeper. "That's not good."

She looked at me sideways. "Was it like that with you and Oliver?"

I breathed out a little laugh. "Oh, not at all. Oliver would come to my house if I didn't message him back quickly or if I didn't answer his calls."

"God, I wish Gray would be more like that. I feel sometimes like I'm the only one trying, you know?"

"That's not how things are supposed to be, Gilly."

She sighed. "I know. I should break things off, shouldn't I?"

I put my arm around her shoulders. "I know it's hard. But it's probably for the best."

I probably needed to take my own advice. I knew that things between Oliver and I weren't real, that they wouldn't last. We'd only hooked up a couple of times, and he clearly still held some resentment toward me. Hell, I held some resentment toward him, as well.

Gillian sniffled, a single tear sliding down her face. She was always bubbly and happy, so when it came to negative emotions, she liked keeping it short and sweet.

"Tell me about Oliver. How things were for the two of you back then."

I let out a long breath, a small smile spreading across my face. "He was... intense. That's the only word to explain it. When he kissed me, when he touched me, it was like we were the only two people in the world."

"Was it love at first sight?" she asked, her eyes widening, and I kicked myself for not having these kinds of conversations with her when she was younger.

She needed a big sister to tell her what love was like, so that she wouldn't look for it in the wrong places.

"Not for me," I admitted. "It was at the Pig. On the dance floor."

"Is that where you met?"

I nodded, smiling. "I was out with my friends, dancing, celebrating someone's birthday or something, I don't remember. Anyway, I saw Oliver outside chatting with a friend, and the way his eyes followed me, it was as if he'd seen me before, recognized me. But I didn't know him. I mean I had seen him at school, but I didn't pay much attention, you know? I wasn't a cool kid, and he totally was."

"Did you think he was cute?"

"Gorgeous," I breathed. "He had the deepest brown eyes, broad shoulders. But I never thought a guy that looked like him would go for a girl who looked like me. So I didn't think much else about it, not until I was on the dance floor."

"I can't believe the Pig used to have a real dance floor

instead of patrons having to move around the pool tables," she giggled.

"Mmm-hmm, used to have a disco ball and everything," I laughed. "But anyway, he grabbed me by the hip and turned me around."

"That's so romantic," she squealed. "Did he say anything?"

"He said 'wanna dance?' I nodded, and he gave me the sexiest, slowest smile."

"That sounds wonderful," she said, her tone bittersweet. "I wish I had something like that with Gray. We worked together for months on campus before I got the courage to ask him if he wanted to go out. *I* had to ask *him*."

"Love isn't always instant," I told her. "Sometimes it grows. And maybe it will with Gray, but if not, there are—"

"Don't you dare say there are plenty of fish in the sea."

"Other guys who could love you better, is what I was going to say," I finished, smiling at her. I noticed Gillian's eyes were a bit wet.

"I've missed you, sissy," she whispered, and pressed her forehead to mine.

In that moment, at least, I was glad I came back to Wagontown.

Chapter 14

Oliver

I headed down to the cabin once I was sure Trent was sleeping. It was shortly after seven-thirty, his bedtime, and I had great news for Lexie.

As I got closer to the cabin, I noticed she was just getting in and I frowned.

Where had she been?

Jealousy initially rushed through me, but when I realized that she was wearing what appeared to be sweats, I pushed it away. Surely, she wouldn't have dressed that way for a date.

It's none of your business.

She could have been out shopping or something, for all I knew. But she didn't have any grocery bags.

It doesn't matter.

I gritted my teeth, working hard to push images of Lex and Tristan out of my head. Then I remembered seeing her at Bonnie's, and I felt stupid.

She'd been out with her little sister.

Lex was startled as I approached. I immediately put up my hands and gave her a smile.

"Not a robber, I promise."

She laughed a little at the joke then let herself inside. I followed, closing the door behind me.

"I have some great news," I told her, grinning. "I officially bought the Pig."

Her green eyes widened. "You didn't say you were buying the Pig."

I laughed. "I wanted it to be a surprise."

"Why the Pig?"

I shrugged. "Clayton has been trying to sell for years, and the place makes a good profit. It's a good business, especially in the summer."

"Tourists," she said derisively, and I laughed.

"Tourists. They're good for business, coming here and playing cowboy."

"As opposed to being a real Wagontown cowboy?"

"I ride the oil rigs, don't I?" I teased, stepping closer to her. She turned to look at me, bracing her hands on the kitchen island.

Her mouth parted and I wanted to kiss it. But this wasn't the time.

I cleared my throat instead. "I want you to work your first shift tomorrow night."

She bit her bottom lip. "Hmm. I must admit, I expected I'd have longer to do some research. I've never poured alcohol professionally."

I chuckled. "And I've never been a bar owner. We'll learn together. Besides, Clayton has some of the best staff in the world."

"That's true. For a dive bar, they make a mean mojito, among other things," she admitted, smiling at me.

"How were the wings?" I asked.

"To die for, just like you said."

105

God, her mouth looked so inviting. Trent could sleep through an elephant stampede, but I didn't like leaving him alone in the house for long, just in case.

"I gotta go," I said. "I'll see you at the Pig tomorrow, let's say five p.m."

"See you then," she murmured, and I tore my eyes away from her, heading out of the cabin and back up to the house before I could change my mind.

I tried to cool my rushing blood on the way back. I peered into Trent's room as soon as I got home. He was sleeping like the baby he still was in my eyes.

At five years old, he was starting to get a little sassy, but only in the cutest of ways.

I wondered how Lex was with kids. When we were teens, we'd never been around any, and Trent had been asleep while she was here. But she'd always loved kids, always cooing at them whenever we spotted them while we were out in public, so I assumed she'd be great with them.

I just knew she'd be a great mother.

But she wasn't Trent's mother, and I'd do well to remember that. I'd also do well to remember what she did with Tristan, how it had torn me apart.

I took in a deep breath and headed to my room to take a hot shower, hoping I wouldn't dream about Lex.

The preparations involved before opening the bar was a surprising amount of work, and I watched with wide eyes as Krista, who had become head bartender in the past few weeks, bustled around, getting everything set up.

"No wonder you guys get here early," I muttered. It was

only three in the afternoon, and we didn't open for a couple of hours.

"The kitchen gets here at one," she said flatly. "You're late."

I blinked at her. "Is everything okay, Krista?"

She sighed heavily, her shoulders slumping. "It's just that... you took over the place so quickly and some of us are worried about our jobs."

"Oh, no," I said without hesitation. "That was one of Clayton's hard lines—I was to keep on all of the staff. Besides, I wouldn't have a clue what I was doing without you."

Krista smiled. "So I'm not going to get fired?"

"Absolutely not," I promised. Then I paused. "But I did hire a new bartender. She doesn't have much experience, though."

Krista raised an eyebrow. "Girlfriend or sister?"

I stared at her. "Neither."

She hummed. "We'll see. What's her name?"

"Lexie," I answered, and she nodded.

"Tell her to find me when she gets here. I'll start training her tonight. It's a Monday, so it'll be slow."

"I'll pay you a training wage," I promised her, and she grinned.

"Maybe this buyout won't be so bad after all."

For the next couple of hours, I walked around, observing the bar and the kitchen staff, watching how things were run. I wanted to get to know what I was working with, how things operated in what I now owned.

By the time Lex arrived, dressed in a simple A-line skirt and a sleeveless blouse, I thought I had gotten the gist of it.

"Find Krista," I told her as she walked in. "You'll be training with her tonight."

"Yes, sir," she mumbled, but I spotted a small smile in the corner of her mouth and my heart skipped a beat. She always looked so beautiful when she smiled.

I cleared my throat as I headed back to the office, continuing to observe the staff as they worked. I had already noticed that Krista was a steady and hard worker, buzzing around like a busy bee. She was patient with Lex as she trained her, showing her the ropes, and Lex seemed to pick up on it quickly.

She followed Krista closely, mimicking her steps, and I could tell that she was already doing a great job.

Within a couple of hours, Krista was slammed at the bar, every seat full, and Lex picked up the slack, tending to the few stragglers at the end of the bar and even some of the tables.

Krista came to the office for a brief moment to make change. I looked at her curiously as she counted out the bills.

"What do you think of the new girl?"

"Lexie? Oh, she's great, boss. She's getting the hang of it quickly. She may be new to all of this, but I think she'll be a hard worker," Krista said brightly before hurrying off to give the customer his change.

Around midnight, it started to get a little rowdy. Krista approached me twice about cutting off a couple of regulars, and I gave her the go ahead. I knew that she could tell better than me when someone was three sheets to the wind.

Liquor licenses were fragile, and they involved a lot of liabilities if we overserved, so I trusted my head bartender, just as Clayton had.

The only snafu happened when a regular got belligerent when asked to leave. His name was Greg, and he wanted another beer after getting cut off. When he was denied, he started cursing at Lexie and Krista.

I came out of the office upon hearing the commotion and tapped Greg's shoulder.

"Excuse me," I said in a low tone, ready for a fight.

Greg whirled around and even though he was probably fifty pounds heavier than me and just as tall, he stopped short, blinking when he saw me.

"Oliver? Oliver Stanhope? What the hell are you doing at the Pig?" he asked, his eyes glassy.

"Oh, you haven't heard?" I asked cheerfully. "I bought the place off Clayton, couple of weeks ago. Today is our grand opening."

"I don't give a fuck about a grand opening," Greg slurred. "I want my beer."

"You can pick up a six pack on your walk home," I told him, leading him toward the door.

"Clayton would have given my keys back and given me a beer," he muttered, but he let me lead him to the door anyway.

"I doubt that, but you can be sure to complain to him next time you see him," I said, calling Greg a taxi to make sure he got home all right.

Greg Wilson was no stranger to the Pig in the Poke, and he was on the list of regular alcoholics that Clayton gave me to watch out for. The list included mostly men and a couple of women who were barflies and had the tendency to overdo it.

Greg was at the top of the list, and I wished he hadn't waited until my grand opening night to go off the rails. In the end, though, he got into the cab, and everything cooled off, no harm done.

By the time I got my bearings back after that, Krista was

announcing last call. I asked for a rye whiskey Old Fashioned which Lex made, bringing it to me, ducking her head almost sheepishly.

"It's my first Old Fashioned," she admitted.. I took a hesitant sip as she watched me with wide, expectant eyes.

The bitters bloomed on my tongue, the orange and cherry flavors coming right after, and I hummed in pleasure. "It's delicious, Lex."

"Really?" she gasped, bouncing a little on her heels excitedly. "I'm so glad."

"You're doing great," Krista said, coming up behind her. "But I need your help with restocking the beer."

"Got it," Lex replied, shooting me a shy smile while the butterflies in my stomach fluttered relentlessly.

Krista raised an eyebrow, seeming to notice there was some kind of energy between me and Lex but she didn't mention it.

At least not right then.

It was nearly three in the morning by the time the bar was clean and ready to close. I yawned so wide my ears popped.

"It's tough getting used to second shift," Krista said with a chuckle. "But you'll get there."

I rubbed a hand over my face, feeling the weight from lack of sleep.

"I sure hope so. I feel like garbage."

"Me too," Lex admitted, holding her lower back as Krista split her tips with her. Lex's eyes widened as Krista pushed bills into her hand. "I didn't make this much."

"Sure you did. You helped me out a lot, so you get half the spoils. Just make sure you tip out the bussers. They work hard too."

Lexie nodded, looking at the money in her hand as if it

were spun gold. She walked over to the bussers, giving them a few bills each for their trouble.

"I have to learn tip-out culture," I murmured, and Krista nodded.

"The golden rule is two to three percent of your sales, but I usually wing it. The bussers make a wage but they deserve tips when they do a good job."

"What about the kitchen?" I mused, wondering how far it went.

Krista shrugged. "Sometimes I'll throw them a ten for making me some food on the fly. They get paid a lot more than us bartenders, though, so we don't do a percentage for them."

Restaurant culture was turning out to be fascinating, and I wanted to learn more. Krista seemed like the right choice for head bartender and trainer.

"I'm giving you a raise," I said, and Krista balked at me.

"What do you mean, a raise?"

"I'm going to pay you fifteen dollars an hour, plus tips."

"*Plus tips?*" she gasped. "That's crazy, boss—"

"Maybe so, but you basically run this place," I said firmly. "You deserve it, Krista."

"Jeez Louise," she breathed. "I can't wait to tell my husband. Reggie will flip his lid. He's always telling me I don't make enough at this dump."

"Tell Reggie this dump is under new management, and we're going to take care of all our employees," I said with a smile.

Krista smiled back, taking her tips, and giving me a sloppy salute at the door as she left.

The only people that remained were me and Lexie.

"Let me take you home." I offered, and she flushed.

"Thanks. I wasn't looking forward to fooling with a ride

share app." She headed toward the door, and I followed, watching the curve of her ass in that tight skirt.

"How did you do?" I asked, trying not to look at how her ass jiggled.

"I think Krista gave me too much in tips," she hedged. "I made almost three-hundred dollars."

I chuckled. "I think that's average for a night like tonight. We were slammed for a Monday." I locked the door and the two of us headed to the parking lot.

She smiled as she slid into the passenger side of my truck. "I can't imagine what I could make on a Saturday night."

"Does that mean you'll stay?" I asked softly, and I didn't mean just for the week.

"For a while," she answered hesitantly, looking out the window.

Stay forever, I wanted to say, but I kept my stupid mouth shut.

I drove her back to the cabin and walked her to the door.

"I can't believe how tired I am," she nearly whispered, looking up at me, biting her lower lip.

"Me, too," I confessed, looking down at her mouth. Trent was staying the night at his grandmother's house, so I didn't have anyone to go home to.

"I was just thinking about that time that we went to the movies and my folks were supposed to be gone, but they came back early from their trip," Lexie said with a chuckle.

I grinned at her. "Yeah, we had plans for me to stay over."

She giggled again. "I thought you were going to get stuck in the basement window. Who knew your butt was that big?"

I laughed loudly, remembering our mutual panic when

I could only get one half of my butt through the window into the basement and I had been briefly stuck hanging above the basement floor, with one leg tangled in her mom's rose bushes.

"That turned into a pretty fun night, as I remember it," I said quietly, looking at her beautiful face in the moonlight. She looked exactly the same as she had that night when I had known I should just go home, but couldn't convince myself to do so.

"Yeah, once we got your booty through the window," she reminded me.

"That's the good part about being adults," I said to her, leaning closer. "We don't have to sneak around anymore."

I leaned my head down and kissed her, and she moaned into my mouth. I knew she was as lost in this as I was, and I didn't care anymore if it was right or wrong.

Chapter 15

Lexie

I expected the sex to be rough and dirty, but when we got inside, Oliver pulled away, taking my hand and leading me to the bathroom.

I went limp as he sat me down on the toilet and started a hot bath. He undressed and got in first, then I shed my clothes, stepping in and sitting in front of him. He put his arms around me, my back against his bare chest.

He'd raided my cabinet for bath salts and bubble bath. The water smelled amazing and felt even better on my sore muscles. Oliver took a wet cloth and started to wash my legs, my thighs, my abdomen, eventually moving to my breasts, which made me gasp.

But he didn't linger, disappointing me slightly.

He washed my back, my hair, cleaning himself as he did so. He pampered me, massaging my shoulders as we sat in the hot water.

By the time the water was cold, my fingers and toes were pruning.

"Time to get out, sweetheart," Oliver murmured against

my bare shoulder, and God, it felt like I was back in time instantly.

Oliver had always been good at pampering me whenever I was sick, tired, or just plain down in the dumps. He always knew exactly what I needed, anticipating it before I even had to ask.

That was one of the things that made him such an amazing boyfriend. If it weren't for his trust issues....

But he still had those so it didn't matter. I could enjoy the moment for now, but I had to remind myself that it wouldn't last forever.

Oliver got out of the bath, and I followed on slightly shaky legs. I wasn't used to so much standing and walking around. The night had been good and bad in many ways, but I found I liked the fast-paced environment.

And I *really* liked the extra money. If I could make this much or more every shift, I'd be able to get out of Wagontown a lot faster than I had thought.

Oliver led me into my bedroom and hesitated slightly at the door, a towel slung low over his hips.

"Can I stay tonight?"

"If you don't mind hearing me snore," I joked, and Oliver laughed.

"Never bothered me before."

"You teased me about it enough," I argued, and Oliver grinned as he climbed into bed with me.

He drew me into his arms. "You do snore like a bear, but you're pretty, so I let you get away with it," he mumbled.

I nuzzled against his neck, feeling for all the world like I'd never left his arms. This was dangerous. I knew that I should pull away, ask him to leave.

But if this was all it was, shouldn't I enjoy it? There

could never be anything else between us, not after what happened, but at least I had this moment right now.

It was only a few minutes before I fell asleep.

When I woke several hours later, the sun was high in the sky, and I was sure it was late. I reached for Oliver but found only empty sheets. I sat up, frowning and feeling disappointed, but I didn't know what I expected.

He had a son to go back to. A family.

I took a deep breath, trying not to feel upset, and headed to the bathroom to wash my face and brush my teeth.

When I padded down to the kitchen, the smell of bacon hit my nose and I perked up.

But sadly, Oliver wasn't downstairs, shirtless, making me breakfast. He'd already made me a plate, covering it with a paper towel and leaving a note.

Eat up. - O

I sighed, wishing he was still here as I sat down and started to eat my bacon and eggs—over easy—just how I liked them. He remembered.

Things like that shouldn't make my heart soar but they did. Which was why I had to end all of this.

Not only was he my ex, he was my neighbor, and now, also my boss. Things had always been too complicated but this was getting ridiculous.

My phone buzzed on the table, and I picked it up without looking at the screen.

"Hello?"

"There you are," Gillian said, all in one breath. "I haven't heard from you in days."

I blinked. It had only been three days, what was she so worried for? We didn't talk for years.

"Sorry," I mumbled. "I've been busy. I started a new job, you know, the one Oliver offered me."

"Oh, that's right! Do you still have the job at the store? Thought you liked it there."

"I do. The Pig is just a second gig, to earn more money."

"My sister, the bartender," she crowed. "Does that mean you could slide me free drinks if I come down on Thursday nights?"

"Maybe a couple of beers," I hedged. "So what's up? You seem a little... manic."

"Well, I got dumped before I could do the dumping," she admitted. "And I guess I've been feeling a little restless. I wanted to know if you wanted to go shopping."

Shopping could be dismal when you only had twenty bucks to spend, but the time with my sister might be fun.

"All right. Where are we going?"

"Wilmington, of course!"

I scoffed. "I can't afford anything in Wilmington, Gilly."

"My treat," she said. "I got a promotion at work and I've got money to burn. *Please*, Lex. I need this."

"All right, but only if we can have brunch and mimosas and not have to drive."

"Perfect. My neighbor offered to pick us up anytime we need it. I can grab my car tomorrow." Gillian sounded excited, and her exuberance was contagious. I smiled.

"See you in a bit."

"Half an hour. Be ready!" she chirped and then hung up the phone.

I finished my breakfast, slamming down a cup of coffee to wake up a little bit. It was a rare day off for me from both jobs, so why not do it up with my sister?

It's been nice getting to know her all over again. I'd

judged her too harshly before. It wasn't her fault that she was our parent's favorite.

Parents shouldn't have favorites, anyway.

I dressed in a simple pair of high-waisted shorts, a cute tank, and casual flats and put my hair up in a high ponytail. I headed out to her car with a smile when she beeped the horn in front of the cabin.

As we were leaving, I spotted Oliver at his pool with Trent, the little boy doing a cannonball and yelling for his father to watch. But Oliver's eyes were on me.

A shiver ran down my spine and I waved briefly as we drove past.

She looked at me sideways. "What was that?"

"What do you mean?" I asked innocently.

"That was Oliver, right? He waved at you."

I shrugged. "So? People wave all the time," I said flatly.

Her eyes narrowed. "There's something more going on than what you've told me so far, and I want to know what it is at brunch."

"Shopping first," I pleaded. "I need a new pair of shoes for work."

Gillian's face softened. "Of course. You should have mentioned it before now."

"I didn't want to be a bother. You've already offered me so much."

"And you didn't take it, so this, you have to," she said firmly as she pulled out onto the highway.

The drive to Wilmington, the next town over, was blissfully filled with small talk. It was nice, chatting with Gillian. I should have reached out to her years ago, but Dick had isolated me from my family and friends. In fairness though, my relationship with Gillian was already strained, at least on my end, so I couldn't completely blame that one on him.

I didn't even notice how bad things were until I was away from him, away from the relationship. It was like I was stuck in this little bubble with him, and everything else faded away.

I supposed I just thought that was what love felt like. I certainly felt that way with Oliver, but it'd been a different kind of bubble, one filled with smiles and laughter and love-making, not criticism and insults.

We arrived at a department store in Wilmington, a place where we'd loved to come as kids, and we walked immediately to the shoe section.

I picked out a pair of comfortable shoes, groaning as I tried them on.

"These are going to be so much better, and I can wear them to both my jobs," I said excitedly.

Gillian frowned. "I don't know how I feel about you working so hard all the time," she admitted. "I worry about you."

"It's all right, Gilly. The hours add up to one full-time job, I'm not overworking myself." I wasn't exactly lying. The hours added up to around fifty a week, which was just a little more than a full-time job, but I needed to save up and get out of Wagontown before everything started to fall apart all over again.

Gillian hummed, sounding like she was still on the fence, but then I pointed out a pair of low-heeled boots I knew she'd love, and the subject was instantly changed.

We spent another couple of hours shopping, and Gillian forced me to pick out a couple of fun outfits I could wear to work. Of course, I had the grocery store t-shirt to wear to the store, but there was no strict uniform for the Pig, and I found a pair of cute black shorts and a classy, but sexy, white top that I thought would look nice.

Looking nice meant better tips, Krista had said, so I was going to try and look my best.

The brunch spot was a place simply called Bacon and Mimosas—two of my favorite things.

Gillian was all but drooling as she looked at the menu. "I skipped breakfast."

I grinned to myself, not wanting to tell her that Oliver had cooked me breakfast. I hadn't revealed that he had stayed over last night, and I wasn't sure if I was going to.

Based on what she said earlier, I was sure she was going to try and get it out of me, though.

"Tell me what happened with Gray," I said after we had our first sips of our mimosas.

Gillian sighed heavily. "I was going to break things off. I really was. But then he called and wanted to come over. He was being so sweet..."

"And you hooked up again," I said dryly.

She groaned. "Yeah, exactly. And then after, like some messed up pillow talk, he told me that he was seeing someone else, and it was getting serious."

"Oh, my God," I breathed. "What an absolute ass."

"I know, right? So of course, I kicked him out of my bed and out of my life." She paused, looking down into her half-empty mimosa glass. "He's still calling me, though."

"Do you answer?"

She shook her head. "I have more dignity than that. So, what's it like, working for your ex-boyfriend?"

I blinked. "It's not so bad."

"And he's your neighbor," she pointed out.

"He is," I said slowly, taking a bite of my avocado toast.

"Look, Lex, I'm just going to ask you flat out." She said,

and then took a deep breath. "Are you going to keep hooking up with Oliver Stanhope?"

I winced, not wanting to answer but knowing I had to. "Yes, probably," I admitted quietly, and Gillian gasped.

"This is big, Lex. Really big."

I sighed. "You already knew we hooked up."

"Yeah, but I didn't know you were *still* hooking up!" she exclaimed. "Last thing I heard you were going to break things off."

"I didn't say that, exactly," I hedged.

"Lexie, you know you're playing with fire."

"I do," I said, huffing out a breath. "He stayed over last night. Made me breakfast this morning."

Her eyes widened. "That sounds like more than just hooking up."

"Doesn't it?" I sighed heavily. "He's confusing me. Because I know that he doesn't want a real relationship with me."

"How do you know that?"

"Come on, Gilly. You know how things ended. How angry he was."

"But that wasn't your fault—"

"Wasn't it though? There was something about me that made him not trust me."

Gillian frowned. "I think he was just young. Insecure."

"Maybe," I muttered. "But I'm not sure whether or not anything has changed since then. I don't need to be dating another person who tries to control me. I get to have friends, even if they are men."

"He grew up," she pointed out. "And so did you."

I shook my head. "Maybe, but that doesn't mean we can be together now. He has a son, a whole other life. I'm a much different person than I was back then. I honestly just want to save money and get the hell out of here."

Gillian looked slightly hurt. "Will you call me and keep in touch?" she asked softly. "When you go?"

"Oh, Gilly." I reached over and took her hand. "Of course I will. I promise not to cut you out anymore."

She sniffled. "That's good. Because I need my big sister."

"And I need my little sister," I replied with a warm smile.

In the end, we didn't drink much and didn't need a ride home after all.

I looked out the window as Gillian drove us back to Wagontown, feeling a sense of nostalgia wash over me.

Did I really want to leave here? For good?

Chapter 16

Oliver

After a couple of weeks, I was finally getting the ins and outs of running a bar. I had to admit that I missed Lexie, since she had a couple of days off to work at the grocery store during the busy season. I thought about calling my grandmother, asking how she was doing, but I figured that would be too obvious.

My grandmother could be nosy.

I was beyond surprised when my father walked in, looking around at the things I'd added—more pool tables on the far side, a few more TVs, dartboards, and another bar upstairs.

He whistled low in his throat as I approached him. "This place is more than just a dive bar now, Ollie."

I flushed with pride. "You really think so?"

"I do," he said quietly.

"Can I get you something?' I asked hesitantly, not sure if he was drinking again or not.

"A ginger ale would be great."

I let out a breath of relief. I didn't want Dad getting drunk and sloshy at my bar. I hailed Krista and she made him a ginger ale with lime, sliding it across to him with a smile and a wink.

Dad blushed a little. Krista was way too young for him, but she was a bit of a flirt.

Thankfully, Lexie wasn't like that on her shifts. She was polite and efficient, but she didn't take up a lot of time talking to customers like Krista did. Though that was part of what made Krista such a good bartender, I was glad that Lex didn't do that, because I was pretty sure my blood pressure would be through the roof if she flirted for tips.

"How's everything going?" Dad asked as I sat down next to him at the bar.

"It's going great. Already turning a profit," I said proudly. "Of course, I'm still paying for the renovations, but..."

"Of course," he said. "It seems like you're drawing in a lot of tourist business."

"That's the plan."

He smiled. "I'm proud of you, son." He paused for a long moment. "Have you spoken to your mother recently?"

"Sure." *She didn't mention you.*

"Is she... how is she?" he asked hesitantly.

I plastered on a fake smile. "She seems to be doing great, Dad."

"Good." He cleared his throat. "That's good."

Lexie walked through the doors, and when I looked up to see her coming, I winced and excused myself from the bar.

I rushed toward her, not wanting Dad to know she was working here.

"What are you doing here?" I hissed.

She blinked at me. "Picking up my paycheck? Why?"

"I would have brought it to you."

"Gillian gave me a ride."

I hurried to the office to grab her paycheck, bringing it back and pushing it discreetly into her hands.

"Why are you in such a hurry to get rid of me?" she asked. I winced once more as my father walked up to us.

"Nice to see you again, Alexandra," my father said flatly. Lexie's eyes met his, her own widening in surprise.

"You too, Mr. Stanhope," she replied flatly.

After that, she turned tail and scurried out of the bar. I watched her go and sighed.

"What was she doing here?" Dad demanded to know.

I sighed. "She works here, Dad."

"You gave your ex-girlfriend a job?" he asked incredulously.

I shrugged, feeling defensive. My shoulders stiffened. "I needed a back-up bartender. She needed a job."

"She's already working for your grandmother," he stated in an accusatory manner, and I stared at him, shocked. She was my maternal grandmother, so I was surprised he knew that. Perhaps he saw her during one of her shifts at the store.

"Why does it matter, anyway?" I huffed.

"Because, Oliver," he said in a low tone as he followed me back to the bar, "I know what she did to you. I don't want you to have to go through that again."

"I won't," I said flatly. "That's all water under the bridge." Why did I keep saying it like that? It was like a mantra I was using to make myself feel better about... everything to do with her.

"Is it?" he asked softly, looking at me intently.

I rolled my shoulders around, feeling suddenly tense. "It is," I said firmly. "There's nothing to worry about."

I wasn't actually so sure about that.

My father was right, of course. I'd been hooking up with

Lexie and everything was starting to get confusing all over again. I hated the way it felt—the yearning when I wasn't with her all the time, the jealousy that bubbled up whenever I thought of her dating someone else.

I couldn't ask her to be exclusive yet there was no part of me that wanted to end it. I only wanted more of her as time went on.

I knew I was playing with fire and expecting not to get burned.

Dad kept looking at me like he didn't believe me.

"Do you want another ginger ale?" I asked, clearly trying to change the subject. He sighed heavily.

"You are more than capable of making your own decisions, son, but just remember what it was like before."

"How could I forget?" I snapped.

My father looked away, and guilt washed over me. I'd blamed him for a long time, deep down, because he was the one that told me the truth about Tristan and Lexie. It wasn't his fault that it happened but having him tell me had been a serious blow.

"Dad, why didn't you like her? You were always so hard on her, but when things were good, she made my life have meaning." I eyed him carefully, trying to glean information from his stoic expression.

My father sighed. "She distracted you, son," he admitted. "You were crazy over her and you guys were just kids. I was afraid that she'd get pregnant and you'd forget about all your plans. And... she was just... flighty, you know? Unfocused."

I did know, actually. She was still doing that stuff to me. She was always scared of commitment. I knew her family hadn't taught her much about stable relationships, but it had always hurt that she couldn't be direct with me about her plans for the future. It had hurt that she didn't even try to explain what happened with Tristan.

But I also knew that I had been a hothead and that I hadn't really given her a chance to explain anything to me. I had just assumed the worst about her, like my dad had. The thought made my stomach roll. I had been an ass, and I was just now realizing it. But that didn't mean I had to forgive her for cheating on me, or up and vanishing one day without a word.

"Look," I said. "Krista's got this handled. Why don't we go somewhere to eat?"

Dad shook his head. "I've got steaks marinating at home."

"Well then, you can cook for me," I said, a slight smile slitting his face.

"If you're sure you're not needed here..."

"I'm sure," I said quickly, throwing a sloppy salute at Krista. She smiled, nodding. I knew she'd call if she needed anything.

I followed my father back to his place. Upon entering, I noticed it was suspiciously clean.

"Did you hire someone?" I asked.

He snorted. "No. I can clean up after myself."

I was surprised but also proud. Especially since it seemed obvious that he'd quit drinking. He didn't exactly have a problem, but he certainly leaned on it too much when he and my mom split up.

"You seem to be doing great, Dad. Have you thought about getting back on the market?"

He stared at me. "You're not suggesting what I think you're suggesting."

I laughed. "Why not?"

"Your mother and I—"

127

"Have been separated for nearly a year," I interjected gently. "Maybe it's time to move on."

My father went quiet, and I almost felt bad about bringing it up. "I'm just not ready, Ollie."

"I understand."

He looked at me sideways. "Does this mean that she's moving on? Seeing someone else?"

I groaned. "Dad, don't do that. Don't jump to conclusions."

He sighed. "I know it's none of my business, but I can't help wanting to know."

"I honestly don't know, Dad. She's kept to herself for the last few months. I haven't heard anything."

He headed to the kitchen and grabbed the steaks before going to the patio and tossing them on the grill. While he grilled outside, I made the baked potatoes and vegetables inside.

By the time it was all done, my mouth was practically watering.

My steak was cooked to a perfect medium rare, and I moaned when I put the first bite in my mouth.

"It's good, right?" my dad asked, smiling, and I nodded, slicing once more into the delicious piece of meat.

"You've always been the grill master."

He chuckled. "Your mom always thought so."

There it was. The silence after he said that was awkward and uncomfortable. The thing was, everything always came back to Mom whenever I hung out with Dad. No matter what it was we were talking about.

And it wasn't like I could easily change the subject. What was I going to tell him? That despite how he'd warned me that she was unfaithful years ago, I was sleeping with Lexie again?

That wouldn't go over well.

And maybe Dad was right. Maybe I was being stupid about this whole thing.

"What do you have for dessert?"

He grinned. "Ice cream."

"Vanilla?" I asked, wrinkling my nose.

"Chocolate for you," he pointed out. "I keep it just in case you come over."

I was a certified chocoholic. I hurried to the freezer, making my dad a bowl of vanilla and a bowl of chocolate for myself.

We chatted idly about my dad's retirement, fishing, golfing, and my new ownership of the Pig. It was nice being able to just chat with him without him asking a million questions about Mom.

She didn't wear her heart on her sleeve like Dad did. She often kept to herself, even when she might need someone to lean on.

After helping clean up, I hugged my father goodbye, promising to be in touch again soon, then headed to my mother's house to pick up Trent. When she came to the door, she looked a little flustered.

"Oh no, has he been a hellion?" I asked with a chuckle.

She frowned. "Of course not. He's always an angel."

"You look tired, that's all."

"That's not a nice thing to say to a lady," she huffed.

I reached out and put a hand on her shoulder. "Mom, if you need to talk—"

"I'm fine," she replied quickly, gathering Trent's things and placing them into his bag before pushing it into my hands.

"All right," I said as I turned to put his bag in the car.

When I returned, she was holding Trent, who was fast asleep.

Disappointment rushed over me. I was hoping he'd be awake so we could watch a movie or something. With the hours I'd been working lately, I hadn't been able to spend as much time as I'd like to with him.

Maybe after tourist season, things would calm down.

I took Trent from Mom before kissing her on the cheek and whispering a thank you and a goodbye. I placed him gently into his car seat, made sure he was secured, then headed home.

As I pulled into my driveway, I noticed that Lexie's light was on, even though it was nearly eleven. My first thought wasn't that she had company, but that maybe she couldn't sleep. I supposed she was getting used to bar hours, too.

I ached to go to her.

I was getting in too deep.

The problem was, I didn't know how to stop it.

Chapter 17

Lexie

I woke up early the next morning for my shift at the grocery store, knowing I was going to have a long day. This was a day where I worked a double shift—eight to four at the store, then six to close at the bar.

I made sure to pack granola bars and some electrolyte water, not wanting my sugar to drop in the middle of work. I also ate a good breakfast—whole wheat toast with eggs and a side of sausage I found in the freezer. It was a bit freezer burnt but it would do the trick.

I walked out to the mailbox, but it was just a bunch of junk mail.

"Hey!" a small voice called out.

I frowned, peering with my hand covering my eyes from the sun. "Who's there?"

"A troll under the bridge," the voice giggled, and I couldn't help but laugh.

"There's no bridge! You're homeless!" I exclaimed.

"Nooo," the voice wailed, and soon Trent came into view, his sandy hair mussed from playing in the grass.

"You must be Trent," I said, and the little boy smiled brightly at me, his teeth small and straight.

"That's me," he said proudly, pointing to himself with his thumb. He tilted his head, staring at me. "Who are you?"

"My name is Lex," I said. "I'm a friend of your dad's."

"My dad doesn't have any friends," he said flatly, and I chuckled.

"Well, he's got me. We're old friends, from before you were born."

"Dad had friends before I was born?" he asked, walking up to me.

"Does he know where you are?" I asked, suddenly concerned.

He shrugged. "He knows I'm playing, don't worry."

I looked around but couldn't see any sign of Oliver.

"Maybe we should walk back to the house."

"Aw," he pouted. "I was hoping to see the witch's cabin."

I blinked at him. "The what now?"

"The witch's cabin," he repeated, pointing behind me. "Is that where you live?" His eyes widened. "Are *you* the witch?"

I laughed. "I'm no witch, kiddo. But I do live in the cabin."

"Are you *sure* you're not a witch?" he asked slyly, smiling. He looked so much like his father that I blinked a little. It was kind of confusing to see so many similarities between them. It gave me vertigo a little bit.

I hadn't known Oliver when we were kids. We just didn't run in the same circles. I vaguely remembered him when he was slightly older than this, but I didn't have any concrete memories of him until we were teens.

I wondered if this little boy would also play football, go

hunting with his dad, and prefer going fishing to having a girlfriend until he was thirteen.

"Pretty sure." I wiggled my nose like Samantha from *Bewitched.* "See, nothing happened."

"You have to have a wand," he said, like that was common knowledge. "Haven't you seen any of the Harry Potter movies?"

I shrugged. "I never got my wand in the mail."

"So, can I see inside?" he asked, bouncing around on his heels.

I grinned at him. He was cute, resembling a tiny Oliver but with other features I assumed came from his mother, such as his button nose and dimples.

"Sure, why not? I can give you a quick tour."

We walked inside and he reached for my hand, holding it. I pointed at the kitchen.

"That's where I make all my spells. In a cauldron."

"What's a cauldron?"

"A really big pot," I replied, chuckling as I showed him around. He seemed fascinated but also a little disappointed that there weren't any magic spell books amongst my reading collection.

A knock on the door startled me. I hurried over to it, knowing it must be Oliver.

"Don't worry," I said quickly as I opened the door. "I've got Trent."

"Oh, thank God. I turned my back for *one* minute." Oliver looked frazzled, and I put a hand on his arm to soothe him.

"It's okay, he's fine. He wanted a tour of the witch's cabin."

Oliver groaned. "I keep telling him there's no witch."

"She's the witch," Trent said, giggling. "But she's not a very good one."

"I'm a terrible witch," I said flatly, and Oliver threw back his head and laughed, loud and deep.

"I guess she is," Oliver said, still snickering. "But we gotta go, kiddo. Your grandmother is waiting."

"I wanted to go with you," Trent whined.

I raised an eyebrow, looking at Oliver for answers, and he sighed.

"He wants to go and see the rig. I keep telling him it's too dangerous."

"I'll be careful, Daddy," he promised, his eyes swimming with unshed tears.

God, he was cute. I didn't know how Oliver could ever tell him no.

"Not until you're older, buddy," Oliver said, picking him up. Trent whined for a minute but eventually calmed down. He seemed like a good kid, not prone to tantrums.

"Do you need a ride to the store?" Oliver asked me, and I smiled at him gratefully.

"Yes, I do. Thanks."

I watched as Oliver and Trent walked to Oliver's car, a sedan that I hadn't seen before. I'd only ever seen him driving his truck.

Oliver helped Trent get strapped into his car seat before coming around and opening the passenger door for me.

I put on my seatbelt and turned over my shoulder to find Trent making faces at me. I made them right back, ugly enough to make Trent gasp and giggle.

I stayed quiet as Oliver dropped off Trent at his mother's house. I'd officially met her years ago, but I knew she wouldn't want to see me now. It hadn't gone well when I'd seen his father the other night.

I knew his parents probably hated me after what happened. Hell, I hated myself for the longest time, even though I didn't do anything wrong.

That wasn't what Oliver believed though, and that was the problem. He didn't trust me then, so he damn sure wouldn't trust me now.

I took in a deep breath as Oliver came back to the car, smiling at me. His smile quickly faded, however, when he saw the look on my face.

"Are you all right?"

I plastered on a fake smile. "Sure. Just thinking about what a long day this is going to be."

He whistled. "Having two jobs is a lot. Are you sure you don't want me to reschedule you for the bar tonight?"

I shook my head. "No, I need the money."

"To get out of Wagontown," he said flatly.

I huffed. "Yeah, to get out of Wagontown."

Oliver took off fast onto the highway, as if what I said upset him. I'd never lied to him, and I wasn't about to start now, regardless of what he believed.

All I wanted was to start my life over, away from all these painful memories.

Was that too much to ask?

* * *

My shift at the grocery store went by without incident. I received my paycheck for the week, smiling at Agnes as she gave it to me.

"You're doing great here, Lex. It's good to have the extra help during tourist season."

"I'm happy to do it."

I stopped by the diner and grabbed a sandwich and

fries, eating quickly before my shift at the bar started. I arrived a few moments early to see Krista setting up for a big table.

"Oh, geez," I muttered, and she laughed.

"It shouldn't be too bad. They called ahead to order their appetizers and drinks. We'll just need to deal with refills. Raoul will be manning the bar tonight, and we'll work on this party."

"How many?" I asked, looking around, a little intimidated by all the chairs she'd set up.

"Fifty, fifty-five," she answered, as if that wasn't a ridiculous amount of people for one table.

My eyes widened. "I've never taken a party this big," I explained, but Krista just shrugged.

"You'll have me to help. They're good tippers, don't worry."

I was still new to all this so I did worry. And, of course, I messed up, dropping a tray of drinks while taking them to the table. Raoul was so nice, telling me not to worry about it as he helped me clean it up.

"Thank God," I mumbled as he made the rest of the drinks.

He laughed, the sound low in his chest, sweeping back his dark hair with one hand.

"Don't worry about it, honey. You're still fairly new. I don't expect you to be perfect."

"You're a great guy, Raoul," I told him, and he just smiled. He was handsome and young, I'd say early twenties. I felt like an old lady next to him.

The party only got just a little rowdy, and Krista and I were able to handle it with ease. Both of us were good at turning on the charm, so we did exactly that, some of the older, more inebriated patrons liking our sass, so it all worked out in the end.

We were splitting the tips, sitting cross-legged on the back stoop, when Oliver finally made his appearance.

It was nearly eleven o'clock and he'd been inside the office all night.

"How'd the fifty-top go?" he asked.

"We did fine without you, boss," Krista said coolly, smiling sweetly when Oliver glanced at her.

"We didn't need your help," I egged her on, giggling.

"Look, I'm sorry," Oliver sighed. "I got stuck on the phone with Clayton. He's worried about his staff."

Krista stood up, patting Oliver's shoulder. "Tell old Clayton we're doing great. Making more money all the time."

She handed me my cut, which was around four-hundred dollars, and my eyes widened as I pocketed it.

"And don't ask me if I'm sure," Krista warned me. "You're doing amazing for a first timer."

"I think we're going to close down at midnight," Oliver said with a big yawn. "I'm tired and it's a Tuesday. We're not going to get much more business."

"Sounds perfect to me, boss," Krista said.

"I've asked you to call me Oliver," he said flatly, but Krista just shrugged and went inside, leaving Oliver and me alone.

I stood there awkwardly for a moment.

"I'll go clean up my section," I said finally, and started to walk past, but Oliver grabbed me by the wrist.

"Stay afterward," he said in a low tone. "I'll drive us home."

Oh, boy.

Despite all the alarm bells ringing in my head, telling

me to break things off, I stayed after everyone else left, waiting for Oliver to come out of the office.

Finally, a little after midnight, he did, walking toward me as I sat perched on the edge of one of the pool tables.

He looked at me, smiling softly, his head tilted to one side.

"What is it?" I asked, smiling back.

"Just had the weirdest sense of déjà vu," he explained. "Feels like I've seen you before on that very pool table, perched just like that."

"You probably have," I murmured, starting to hop down, but he came up to me, placing his hands on my hips.

"Don't move," he said in a low voice. "I want to remember you, just like this."

One of his hands moved to trail up my thigh, slipping under the high-waisted shorts I wore, and I gasped at his touch.

"Oliver," I whispered.

"Lex," he whispered back, as he moved his head to kiss my throat, sliding his tongue over my skin and making me shudder all over.

The next thing I knew, he grabbed my hips and placed me on the ground, turning me around with ease and bending me over the pool table.

I wanted to ask about us getting caught, what if someone came back in, what if someone forgot something? But something told me that was what made this as hot as it was so I kept my mouth shut.

He moved his hands to my waistband, unbuttoning my shorts and pulling them down, biting down on the curve of my hip as he did so. I gasped and arched my back as he moved his hands over my ass, finding the curve of my waist to hold onto as he ground himself against me.

He was hard and before I knew it, he'd freed himself and was pushing into me as I spread my legs further apart.

I raised my ass up to meet him, crying out his name when he buried himself to the hilt, whispering against my throat. I could barely hear him.

"I missed this. I missed you."

I pretended I didn't hear what he'd said, pretended it didn't make my heart soar, because I couldn't keep doing this. This *had* to be the last time, and I was going to tell him, as soon as my legs started working again, as soon as...

He thrust into me with long, deep strokes, sliding against my sweet spot in a way that made my breath hitch in my throat. I clawed at the green felt of the surface beneath me, trying to steady myself as my legs grew shaky. Oliver reached up to cup my breasts briefly, throwing off our cadence, and crushing my body against the edge of the table. The sharp jolt of pain mixed with the pleasure, and drew a gasp from my lips.

"Sorry," he said quietly, slowing down for just a moment, as he helped me to step back a little. He slid his hand up the column of my throat, holding on gently while his other hand wrapped around my midsection.

I leaned back against him, angling my hips to take him deeper, imprisoned with him all around me and within me, alight with pleasure that made me shiver and cry out. His long fingers that were wrapped around my throat remained gentle, but firm, even as I started to shake and snap with my impending release.

"Stay with me," he said roughly to me, driving into me harder. "Don't leave me again."

"Oliver," I panted, trying for a placating tone, but failing. I just sounded desperate, brimming over with lust.

"Just stay this time," he said again, his tone holding a note that sounded like a plea.

I didn't answer, I couldn't even if I had wanted to. My orgasm was hovering around the edges of my awareness, threatening to send me to the floor as a shaky, sodden mess. When I finally came it felt like fireworks exploded behind my eyelids. I literally saw stars. Only Oliver had ever been able to make me do that.

Oliver moaned against my ear when he spilled inside me, kissing along my neck, the side of my face, everywhere he could reach.

"Never thought we'd make love in the Pig," I giggled, and Oliver laughed with me before slowly pulling out, steadying me with a hand on my hip.

"Maybe that's why I bought the place," he teased, and I snorted out a laugh as he pulled up my shorts.

I buttoned them, blushing. He pulled up his jeans then adjusted himself as we headed to the door. After shutting down the lights and locking up the place, we walked out to the parking lot.

In the car, I went quiet, mostly to try and think of the right words to say.

"Oliver?" I said when we were halfway home. I bit my lip so hard I tasted copper.

"Mmm?"

"That has got to be the last time, okay? I can't do this anymore."

Oliver was quiet for a moment, his shoulders stiff, but then he shrugged. I couldn't really read his face due to the dark and the way he looked to the side to navigate a turn.

"Okay."

"Okay?"

That was all he had to say? Okay? He had pleaded with

me to stay, begged me to think about staying while we were having sex. Okay?

"Sure. If that's what you want."

"It is," I said, more confidently than I felt, and Oliver just glanced at me. His expression told me nothing at all about what he was thinking. I felt closed off, shut out, and it hurt more than I thought it would.

"Then that's it. It's the last time."

That was it.

Was it really that easy? Why was I so annoyed?

Wasn't this what I wanted? For it to be over?

I was still reeling when he dropped me off at the cabin.

"Wait, Lex," he said, and I quickly turned around, relieved, hoping he'd ask me why, beg me not to break things off. But then he handed me my apron out the window. "Don't forget this."

"Oh. Thanks," I mumbled before he drove away.

What in the hell was *that*?

Chapter 18

Oliver

I left Lexie's cabin feeling disheartened, but at the same time, I knew she was right. I was definitely falling back in love with her, and that was something I couldn't afford to do. It'd nearly killed me the first time.

Instead of going straight home like I'd planned, letting Trent stay over at my mother's house, I headed over to pick him up, feeling lonely. I didn't examine why. I felt like I was in shock, and if I allowed too much awareness of what had just happened to permeate the numbness, I would have a full-on panic attack.

I knew Trent would be asleep, but at least I wouldn't have to be in my big house all by myself. I didn't think I could handle that, not tonight.

My mother came to the door, sleepy and surprised.

"Ollie? What are you doing here so late? I thought you were going to let him sleep over."

"Just missed him, I guess," I muttered. "I've been working so much lately."

My mother looked at me curiously, and I knew she could tell something was wrong.

"Ollie," she said firmly. "Let's talk and have some tea."

I knew that I wasn't getting out of this easily, so I sighed and followed her as she put on the tea kettle. We stood in the kitchen, staring at each other for a few minutes.

"Tell me what's wrong," she demanded, and I huffed out a breath.

"No." She blinked at me in surprise. "Not until you tell me why you left Dad."

I guess I wanted to change the subject so badly that I brought up something I knew she wouldn't want to talk about. Or maybe I truly wanted to know the answer. I thought at first that my parents' separation wouldn't bother me, after all, I'm a grown man. Yet here I was asking my mother for an explanation.

After seeing Dad the other night, I really wanted to know.

She took in a deep breath. "That's none of your business, Oliver."

"Isn't it?" I asked, stepping forward to pour our tea into cups. "It seems like something I should know, Mom."

"It just wasn't working," she said flatly, heading to the table with her tea. She sat down heavily into a chair. I followed and sat across from her. "Your father... he can be a very critical man, you know."

"I do know," I said softly. My father had pushed me to be the man I was today, going out on the rigs and working hard. Now that he was retired, he nitpicked me relentlessly. I guess I never knew that he did it to Mom, too.

"It just got to be too much. There was always something wrong with my cooking or the way I cleaned the house, or the plans I made. I grew tired, Ollie. You shouldn't be constantly tired when you are in love."

I drew in a sharp breath. Tired was precisely how I felt

right now. Tired of fighting my feelings. Tired of pretending I *wasn't* in love with Lexie. If my mother was right, and you weren't supposed to feel tired in love, what was the alternative?

"I messed up, Mom," I said softly, and she reached across the table and took my hand in hers.

"Tell me," she said softly.

Tears burned at the backs of my eyes, but I didn't let them fall.

"I'm in love with Lexie Tripp," I said finally, and she gasped subtly.

"Oh, honey, I knew that already." When I gaped at her, she just smiled. "You've always been in love with her, haven't you?"

"I guess so," I admitted, almost wanting to laugh at the ridiculousness of it all. How could I think I could be with her again and not fall in love with her?

"It was your father who didn't like her, you know," she said. "I thought she was a lovely girl."

"He had reasons not to like her," I muttered.

"Did he?"

My mother's words struck me oddly and I looked at her intently. "Mom, do you know something I don't?"

She shrugged. "Just that your father didn't want to see you with her. I'm not sure what it was though I think it had something to do with her father, and his poor business practices, and her own slightly unfocused nature"

"But what Lexie did with Tristan—"

"I don't know anything about that. All I know is how you looked at her, Ollie. Like she made the world stop turning." She smiled sadly. "Your father once looked at me like that. A long time ago."

"I think you should talk to him, Mom. Tell him how you feel. I think it would make a big difference."

She hummed. "Maybe it will. Or maybe it won't make any difference at all."

I felt the same way about Lexie. Even if I did tell her how I felt, would it matter? She's made it clear she wants to leave Wagontown. When that happens, I'll be heartbroken all over again.

"Why don't you stay here tonight, honey?" My mom suggested. "I'll pull out the couch into a bed, it's pretty comfortable."

My shoulders slumped. "That would be nice," I admitted. I was exhausted, and heartsick to boot.

I lay on the pullout bed, looking up at the ceiling, and thinking about Lexie, wondering if she was looking up at her ceiling and thinking about me.

Probably not. She was probably fast asleep, dreaming about her escape from Wagontown.

* * *

The next morning, I woke to a text from her: *I'm so sorry to ask, but could I get a ride to the bar tonight?*

I frowned at the phone, annoyance trickling through me. I had told her that I'd give her a ride any time, but for her to ask right after she broke things off seemed cruel.

But at the same time, I had made myself available to her with a sincere offer, and that wasn't just because we were hooking up.

I spent the day at my mother's with Trent. We dug out the colored plastic eggs we used at Easter, filling them with candy and money, even though Easter was still months away. Trent got a kick out of looking for them knowing the Easter Bunny was nowhere to be found.

"He'll never guess we're looking!" he snickered, and I couldn't help but laugh at his cute innocence.

"I'll be back in a few hours," I told my mother after several moments of watching Trent search. "I just need to check in at the bar. I won't be out late tonight."

"Good to hear. Trent likes it when he can be tucked into his own bed."

Guilt rushed over me again, but I had to work, and getting this bar off the ground under new ownership meant I needed to be there as often as possible. At least for the first few months.

I kissed and hugged Trent goodbye then headed out to pick up Lexie.

She slid into my truck, frowning slightly. "Where's Trent?"

"With his grandmother," I said flatly, not looking at her as I pulled onto the road. "I'm going to spend a couple of hours at the bar when I drop you off."

"I'm sure Krista and I—"

"I need to do some paperwork," I stated, cutting her off. Lexie shut her mouth. I figured she finally got the hint that I didn't want to talk.

I walked straight into the office and sat down, breathing hard while trying to get my thoughts together. I felt angry seeing her again, angrier than I thought I'd be, and I needed to calm down.

A strange, stifled scream sounded out over the music, and I was up and running out of the office before I knew what was happening.

There was a man standing with his back to me, facing Lexie. She looked terrified.

"Is this guy bothering you?" I asked loudly, and he turned.

"She's my fiancée," he snapped back. It was her ex.

Her controlling ex who'd emotionally abused her. Her ex who she ran away from. I tackled him around the waist, not thinking, and we both went down to the floor.

He got in a couple of body shots before I punched him in the throat and he started to gasp, clawing at his neck.

"Oliver, no!" Lexie exclaimed. "It's not worth it!"

She pulled me off him and he scurried away like a cockroach out the back door. I followed him, my chest heaving, Lexie hanging onto my arm.

When I realized she was shivering and trembling all over, I drew her into my arms, pressing my lips to the crown of her head.

"It's going to be okay," I assured her.

I meant it.

I'd make sure her ex never came anywhere near her again.

Chapter 19

Lexie

I couldn't seem to stop shaking.

"I know it's hard, Lex, but you should call the police. Make sure there's a record of this."

"I don't want to—"

"I know," he said softly, cupping my face in his hands. "But you need a restraining order now that he knows where you work."

I swallowed hard. Oliver was right. I needed to keep myself safe.

I pulled out my phone and called 911, letting them know I'd been harassed and giving them the address of the bar.

Oliver decided to shut down the bar for the night, sending everyone home, and not a soul complained. Krista gave me a quick hug as she left, even Raoul giving me a sympathetic look and a little wave.

"Everything's going to be all right," Oliver repeated, rubbing my back in comforting circles, and I felt glad that he was with me, glad that he protected me.

Reese Cunningham, the sheriff's senior lieutenant, was the first to arrive on the scene.

"My ex has been harassing me," I said quietly. "And he knows where I work now. I would like to get a restraining order."

Lt. Cunningham asked me about a million questions, but in the end, it all boiled down to Dick's full name, last known address, and full physical description.

He then spoke to Oliver for a long moment while I went inside, drinking some soda to try and settle my stomach. It didn't work very well. I felt nauseous, my nerves on edge from the incident with Dick.

"I'm going to keep you safe from him," Oliver promised me after we finished up with Lt. Cunningham and got into his truck. "He's not going to find out where you live."

"I appreciate all your help, Oliver, but you don't have to do all of this—"

"Of course I do."

He dropped me off at the cabin and watched me go inside, staying in the yard for a long time before pulling out, presumably to pick up Trent.

I didn't feel great being there alone, but I knew he'd be back shortly. I went to the couch to lie down, my head pounding, my stomach rolling.

God, how had he found me?

Dick had walked right up to me, and all I could do was stare, shaking.

"What the hell do you think you're doing, dressed like a whore?" he demanded to know, and I realized right away that he was drunk.

Dick didn't drink much, but when he did, he was a totally different person.

"You're coming home," he said brusquely, and grabbed my hand. That's when I screamed.

Oliver had come out of the office like my knight in shining armor. Thank God he'd been there, because Dick may have tried to pull me out of the bar and into his car. God only knows what would have happened then.

I already knew that Dick wasn't the guy I'd originally thought he was. But I'd never thought he was dangerous. However, after his appearance at the bar and seeing the look in his eyes, I was beginning to think differently.

I took in deep breaths, trying not to throw up, but I ended up hugging the toilet anyway.

* * *

I woke up the next morning overwhelmed by nausea. I had a shift at the grocery store and I knew there was no way I was going to make it. After another bout of hugging the porcelain, I called Agnes. She picked up on the first ring.

"I think I ate something that didn't agree with me," I said slowly, trying not to throw up again.

"Oh no," she gasped. "Well, you stay at home and get better, you hear me? I'll ask Oliver to check on you."

"You don't have to do that."

"He won't mind one bit. I'll have him bring you some of my chicken noodle soup. It's got ginger in it. Good for the stomach."

I smiled, thinking she was making too much of a fuss but still grateful, nonetheless. "Thank you, Agnes."

"You're welcome, honey."

I threw up again as soon as I hung up. I was dry heaving at the end of it and I felt awful. Yet somehow I managed to make my way into the kitchen to make some dry toast.

Oliver showed up a half hour later and it was all I could do to answer the door.

"What the hell did you eat so I can stay away from it?" Oliver asked, and I chuckled.

Truth be told, I didn't remember eating much other than a couple of granola bars yesterday, and those had never given me stomach trouble before. Maybe I picked up a virus working at the store or at the bar. Being around people would always end up making you sick, my mom used to say.

"I'm not sure."

"My grandmother sent over her chicken noodle soup. It's got ginger—"

"Good for the stomach," I finished, chuckling. "Thanks. I'll have to put it in the fridge for now. I'll try to eat a little later."

He put it away for me, concern on his face when he walked back into the living room.

"Are you sure you're all right? Do you think this is just from the stress?"

"It might be," I admitted. My stomach was often off when something very stressful happened, so it made sense.

"I'll be watching out for you," he promised, kissing my temple. "I don't want you to worry about anything."

"I'll try not to," I murmured.

After Oliver left, I remembered that I had lunch plans with Gillian. I called her.

"Hello?"

"Gilly, I'm sorry. I'm going to have to postpone lunch," I said hoarsely.

"Oh, no, you sound like hell. Are you sick?"

"Something is off with my stomach," I admitted. "It's been a rough night."

"I'm coming over right now."

"Gillian, you don't have to—" I said weakly, but she had already hung up.

I laid on the couch for another half an hour before she showed up. When I heard her tap on the door, I called out weakly for her to come in.

She hurried inside, holding a bag full of saltine crackers and Gatorade. I smiled at her gratefully.

"Thank you for coming over to take care of me."

"Of course. What are sisters for?" She paused. "Besides, I brought you something that might be useful."

She took a box out of the bag, and I blinked at her.

"A pregnancy test?"

Gillian shrugged. "You never know. I keep a few on hand just to be sure. It could be what's causing this sudden onset of nausea."

"I'm not pregnant," I muttered, but I started doing the math, and realized I couldn't remember the date of my last period. Dick and I hadn't been having sex at the end, given all the stress of planning the wedding, so if I was pregnant, it was Oliver's.

The first thing that happened after that thought crossed my mind, was that I felt elation. I immediately imagined a cute little version of the both of us tugging at my hand and asking to be picked up.

And then reality crashed in on me. I was running from my ex who had tracked me down to Wagontown and threatened me. Oliver and I had a crazy, messed up thing going on. His father hated me. My parents didn't support me.

I was working at a bar and a grocery store and borrowing my house from the man I might be pregnant with. It was all too much, and I started to feel lightheaded.

My breath started to come hard and fast. Gillian sat down next to me, putting her arm around my shoulders.

"It's going to be okay," she tried to comfort me, but I still couldn't seem to catch my breath.

"I can't be pregnant, Gilly."

"Maybe you're not!" she chirped, trying to stay positive for me. "I just thought we should know, one way or the other."

I took in a shaky breath and grabbed the test from her, going into the bathroom to take it.

"It's not doing anything," I complained as I came out, holding the test stick in my hand.

"You have to give it five minutes, Lex. It's not instant," Gillian explained, and I sighed.

I'd honestly never taken one before. I'd always been so careful about keeping up with my cycle so that I wouldn't be caught off guard.

I had known that a possible pregnancy would destroy my dreams of escaping my hometown and bring down the censure of my parents and Oliver's dad. I hadn't even let Oliver kiss me during the times when I might be able to get pregnant when we were sleeping together as kids.

I sat the test down on the coffee table and slumped onto the couch, the next five minutes feeling like three hours. Finally, Gillian picked up the test, her eyes widening.

"Uh..."

"What does 'uh' mean, Gillian?" I demanded to know.

"It's got two lines."

I huffed out a frustrated breath. "And what does that mean?"

She put the test down and looked at me. "It means you're pregnant."

"No," I breathed, sinking farther into the couch as all the oxygen seemed to leave the room. "I can't be pregnant."

"But you are," she said gently. "And we have to talk about what you're going to do."

"I can't talk," I gasped. "I can't even breathe."

Gillian hugged me tightly, rubbing her hands up and down my bare arms. "I need you to calm down, sissy. Breathe in and out, slowly."

It took me a minute, but after a few deep breaths, I started to calm down.

"Ok, so, you're pregnant," Gillian said when we pulled away from each other.

I groaned. "Yes, I'm pregnant."

"And I assume it's Oliver's?"

"Of course it's Oliver's," I snapped. Gillian winced and once again guilt washed over me. I seemed to be getting hit with a tidal wave of it ever since I returned to Wagontown. This wasn't her fault. She was only trying to help, and I needed to calm down. "I'm sorry, honey. It's just... a lot to deal with."

"Of course it is."

"Especially now that Dick showed up."

"Wait. Your asshole ex is in town? When did this happen?" She frowned at me.

"Last night. I just haven't had the chance to tell you. He came looking for me at the bar."

"Jesus," Gillian muttered. "You're really having a rough go of it, aren't you?"

"I am," I whined, leaning against her. "And I feel like if I so much as smell food I'll throw up, but I am hungry."

"Maybe we should try something simple? Like soup?"

"Oliver's grandmother sent over some chicken ginger soup. I could try that."

Gillian nodded, going to the kitchen to heat it up for me.

I took a couple of tentative sips and hunger gnawed at my belly. I started to eat a little faster, noticing my stomach was seeming to settle as I ate.

"They were right about this ginger," I murmured. "Good for the stomach."

Gillian just looked at me, out of the loop, setting off a hysterical laugh. I had no idea what I was going to do about this baby, about Oliver, about Dick, about any of it. The laughter was better than tears. I knew if I started crying there was a good chance I might never stop.

"I'm a little worried about you, sis," she said hesitantly.

I waved my hand dismissively. "Don't be worried. I'll figure it out. I always do."

"You don't have to do this alone." She put her hand over mine, and tears sprang to the backs of my eyes. I fought hard, but I couldn't keep them from falling.

"Thank you, Gilly. For everything."

"Don't say that like you're about to disappear," she said, fear evident in her voice. "You can't just take off."

"I don't know what else to do," I admitted. "I don't really have the funds to start over, but I can't stay here. I'll start to show, and then Oliver will know."

"Shouldn't he know?" she asked quietly. "Oliver has the right to know you're pregnant with his baby."

"I can't tell him. He'll never let me leave Wagontown."

She frowned. "He can't stop you."

"He'd never try to stop me, but he'd work hard at convincing me to stay. He'll tell me the baby is better off having two parents, that they would be more mentally and emotionally stable growing up in a solid home. He'd be right on both accounts, of course, and I'd be stuck here for the next eighteen years."

"Whoa, whoa, slow down. You haven't even thought about whether or not you're going to keep the baby."

I rubbed my stomach, thinking about it. I couldn't imagine not having this baby, now that I knew it existed. As complicated as things were, Oliver and I had been very much in love at one point, and this was proof of that love.

I knew that I would love this baby. So, so much.

But that didn't mean I wanted to get back together with Oliver.

Or did I?

Could this be the string that finally pulled us together? Could I ever trust him to trust me again?

I didn't know. So for now, I had to keep it a secret.

I took Gillian's hands in mine. "I'm going to keep the baby."

She squealed, hurting my ears. "I'm going to be an auntie!"

I laughed. "Yes, you are. But you can't tell anyone. Not yet."

"You're not going to tell Oliver?"

"I can't. Not yet anyway. I need to tell him in my own time," I explained, hoping she would understand.

"Okay. But I get to come with you to the doctor, right?"

"Of course you do." I smiled at her. "You're all I have right now, Gilly."

She hugged me tightly. It was in that moment that I realized how proud and happy I was to have her back in my life, after all those years of resentment. She hadn't deserved any of it.

She was the only person in town I could trust with my secret.

How long it would stay a secret, however, I had no idea.

Chapter 20

Oliver

I went over to Lexie's cabin the next morning to check on her.

Her sister's car was in the drive and a smaller version of Lexie answered the door.

I blinked at her. "Gillian?"

She smiled. "Oliver. Coming over to check on my sister?"

"Exactly. We also, uh, had plans." I wasn't sure how much to reveal, knowing that Lexie liked to keep to herself.

"Ah, yes. The police station. She has to give her statement to the sheriff, right?"

"Right. We both do."

I was also filing a restraining order against her ex so that if he ever showed up on my property, whether it was here or at the Pig, he would immediately be arrested.

"She's still not feeling great, but I know she wants to get this done," Gillian said, seeming happy to be taking care of her sister.

They hadn't always gotten along when they were younger, so I had to admit I was surprised to see her buzzing around the room, cleaning up, before going into the bedroom and then returning with a smile.

"She's getting dressed," Gillian said.

I watched her curiously. "How are your parents?" I asked, not sure how to make small talk with someone I hadn't seen since she was a kid.

"Okay, last I heard," she replied with a shrug. "We don't really talk much anymore."

"I'm sorry to hear that."

"It's for the best," she said, smiling at me. "I want you to know, I'm really grateful that you've been helping Lexie out, giving her a place to stay, a job..."

"She earned it," I said firmly, and I really believed that. Even though she didn't technically pay rent, Lexie had more than made up for that by being so great at the Pig, and at the grocery store. She'd filled two positions that might have taken weeks to fill.

"I'm sure she has," Gillian answered, and she bit her lip as if she wanted to say something else. I was about to ask her what it was when Lexie walked into the living room, looking pale.

I went to her immediately. "Are you okay?" I asked in a low tone.

"I'm fine," she said, her voice raspy. "Just a stomach bug."

I frowned, suspecting more that it was stress than anything else. Lexie had always been susceptible to stress-related illnesses.

"Are you sure you want to do this today? We could reschedule—"

"No," she said firmly, cutting me off before giving Gillian a quick hug. "I want to get it over with." She turned to her sister. "See you next week?"

Gillian nodded, smiling, and then waved at me slightly as she walked out the door. I waved back, feeling a little out of the loop.

"What's next week?" I asked.

"Doctor's appointment," Lexie answered flatly. "Just a checkup, since I got so sick."

I sighed in relief. "That sounds like a good idea."

Lexie was dressed in a pair of jeans and a t-shirt. She looked great in my opinion, her hair swept back from her face with a headband. I wanted to lean down and kiss her, but I hadn't forgotten that she wanted her space. That she'd cut things off.

It still stung.

We walked to the car and I smiled sheepishly, pointing at Trent in the backseat. "My mom is out with friends, so we have to take the rugrat with us."

She laughed. "I never mind him tagging along. Even if he does think I'm a witch."

I snickered. "I think I've got it through his head that you're not."

"Good to know."

I opened the door for her, and she slid inside. As we pulled out onto the road, Trent piped up from the backseat.

"Are we going to the fire station?"

"No, buddy. The police station. And you need to be extra good while we talk to the sheriff."

"Do I get to hear the sirens?" he asked, bouncing in his car seat.

"Maybe," Lexie answered, smiling. "But probably not. It's pretty quiet in Wagontown."

"Aw, man," he whined, but he didn't complain any further and I was grateful.

At the sheriff's office, Reese met us in the lobby. He

looked down at Trent, blinking, and I gave him a sheepish smile.

"No babysitter," I explained.

"That's all right," he said. He turned, calling out for someone named Mariah.

She rushed into the lobby and looked down at Trent, smiling.

"Hello, there. I'm Mariah. What's your name?"

"I'm Trent!" he answered, bouncing on his heels.

"Hi, Trent. How would you like a tour of the station?"

"Do I get to sit in a police car?" he asked, still bouncing. I smiled at Mariah and then down at Trent, finding his exuberance adorable.

"I think that can be arranged," Mariah said, taking Trent's hand and leading him deeper into the office.

Lexie watched Trent with a smile, but I noticed that there was a dullness to her, somehow. I supposed it was because she was sick, but I still hated seeing her that way.

I took her hand as Reese led us into a small room. She didn't react, but she didn't pull away, either. I hated that we'd broken things off before all of this happened. I wanted to comfort her, wanted to be there for her, and I felt like now, I couldn't be.

"Let's start with your statement, Ms. Tripp," he said, and Lexie took in a deep breath.

"It was about six-thirty. I was working at the Pig in the Poke, and my ex, Dick...Richard, came up to me. He called me a name."

"What name?" Reese asked.

"A whore," she said quietly, and my shoulders stiffened. I wished I'd hit him harder. "And then he grabbed me, told me it was time to come home."

"That's when you came in, Mr. Stanhope?"

It felt strange, Reese calling me Mr. Stanhope since he'd only been a year above me in high school, but I allowed it.

"Yeah. I just kind of snapped," I admitted. "I tackled him, and we fought. He got a couple of body shots in, and I returned a few punches myself. When he got up, he ran off."

"I tried to stop the fight," Lexie commented, and Reese nodded, scribbling something down on a notepad.

When he was finished writing, he turned off the tape recorder, and looked directly at both of us.

"I have to be honest with you two. Other than the restraining order, we've got nothing to hold him on."

"What do you mean?" I asked, frowning.

"I mean, the things that happened, they aren't enough to arrest him. Unless he breaks the restraining order, we can't haul him in for nothing."

"But he tried to kidnap her," I argued.

"We don't know that for sure. He said it was time for her to come home, but other than grabbing her hand, he didn't actually try to remove her from the scene." Reese paused. "And if he wanted to, he could actually file assault charges on you."

"He wouldn't!" Lexie gasped.

"He might," Reese countered. "You never know about people, especially guys like that. They try to manipulate every situation."

"Sounds like Dick, all right," Lexie muttered.

I tried to put my arm around her, but she moved away, clearing her throat. Disappointment washed over me.

"That's all for now unless you have any questions. Keep us updated if you see him around town," Reese finished, and I nodded, standing up.

"Don't worry," I murmured to Lexie as we waited for Trent in the lobby. "I'll take care of this."

"Oliver, please don't do anything crazy," she warned.

"I don't know what you're talking about," I replied innocently, although I'd been thinking about hiring a private investigator to find him and run him out of town.

"He could get you in trouble if he decides to file assault charges. You don't need that."

"I want to keep you safe."

"Let the cops do their jobs," she said, but I wasn't sure I trusted the cops. They didn't seem to be taking this too seriously, and I wasn't about to allow Lexie to get hurt.

Trent ran up to us, raising his arms for me to take him. I picked him up, his blue eyes wide with excitement.

"She showed me the sirens," he grinned.

"You're a real police officer now," Mariah said with a wink, giving him a little play badge they probably had on hand for the kids.

I pinned it on his T-shirt and Trent grinned so widely I could see every single one of his teeth.

"Let's get out of here and get some lunch," I said, realizing it was close to noon.

"Could you drop me off at home first?" Lexie asked tiredly, and I frowned.

"You need to eat, Lex."

She didn't argue, she just listlessly walked to the car and got into the passenger seat before I could open the door for her.

What was going on?

"Are you all right?" I asked when we pulled up to the restaurant. She turned to me with a weak smile.

"Just still feeling sick," she admitted.

"They'll have soup or something light," I promised.

We entered the restaurant and sat in a back booth. Lexie ordered a half sandwich and a bowl of broccoli cheddar soup.

She barely ate any of it while Trent chowed down on his double burger. The kid loved meat and couldn't seem to get enough of it. Growing boy, I supposed.

"That's a big burger for a little guy," Lexie pointed out.

"I could eat *two* of these," Trent said proudly, his mouth full, and I nudged him with my shoulder.

"Table manners, Trent."

"Sorry," he mumbled, his mouth still full, and Lexie laughed.

"You're such a good dad," she commented quietly, and there was something almost sad about the way she said it. Was she thinking the same thing I was? That it should have been the two of us with kids, not just me alone?

I knew it was stupid of me to think that way. That wasn't how things were, it was simply how I *wished* things were. Lexie had broken off our recent chance at being together. She didn't want me and it was starting to grate on me, especially since I was trying so hard to help her through this difficult time.

It wasn't that I expected anything in return, but I felt I deserved some sort of explanation as to why she had ended things so abruptly.

I breathed in deeply, knowing we couldn't have this conversation around Trent. Lexie was quiet throughout the rest of the meal, barely touching her food.

She would chat idly with Trent but would basically ignore everything I said.

Anger was starting to roll over me like a tidal wave, and I didn't like the way it felt. I didn't want to be angry with her anymore. I'd been angry for too many years, and it was time to let it go.

"Are you sure you're all right?" I asked again in a low tone while Trent was occupied coloring, and she huffed out a breath.

"I'm fine. I'm sick, Oliver. And you don't have to worry about me. I'm not your problem. Not anymore."

"What is that supposed to mean?" I snapped, unable to quell the anger. I'd been trying to help her all day, and she'd been nothing but cold or downright mean.

"It means you don't have to try so hard," Lexie hissed. "It means you can just take me home. It means you don't have to help me."

"I know that I don't have to help you. I want to, Lex. I care about you."

"Do you? That's news to me." She stood up. "I'll walk home."

Trent looked up at me upon hearing that, his eyes wide. I was angry that Lexie was being difficult, but I was angrier that she'd started this in front of Trent.

"Fine," I said, motioning for the waitress to bring the bill. We sat in silence until it arrived, and I immediately handed the server cash, telling her to keep it. She looked at me in surprise—I didn't want to wait for her to bring back the change, so she ended up getting a very nice tip.

Lexie got up from the table first, storming through the restaurant and out the door. I took my time, waiting for Trent to gather his coloring project and snagging one last fry.

When we got out to the parking lot, I secured Trent in the back then slid into the driver's seat and started the car.

"Daddy," Trent said quietly from the backseat. "We

can't just let her walk home." His voice was small and worried, only making me angrier at Lexie.

I sighed. "I know."

I spotted her stalking down the street, and I drove up next to her, rolling the window down.

"Come on, Lex, I'm sorry. Just get in the car. Let me drive you home."

I didn't want Dick to show up and harass her again. After a minute or two, the thought must have crossed her mind, as well, because she finally got into the car.

"Sorry," she muttered. "I haven't been myself lately."

That's an understatement, I thought but didn't say out loud. I didn't want to worry Trent any more than he already was.

She was reacting to the stress of Dick being in town, and I knew that, but it didn't make her actions and words any less hurtful.

I didn't think I'd ever understand women.

Chapter 21

Lexie

I felt like the world's biggest jerk after I got home, knowing that I'd not only upset Oliver but also Trent. I couldn't seem to control my emotions.

Gillian came to pick me up the next evening. I had a few days off, so I decided to spend them at her place. No matter how hard I tried, I couldn't seem to break the funk I was in.

"You gonna tell me what's got you so down in the dumps?" she asked finally.

I groaned. "I don't know. I just can't seem to bring myself to feel better."

"Physically? Emotionally?"

"Both," I muttered.

"It's hormones," she said easily, and I looked up at her, frowning.

"Hormones?"

"Yeah, most definitely. One of my best friends got pregnant right out of high school, and she was a hormonal mess until the baby was born. She had an attitude every day for nine months, and she couldn't regulate her emotions. The doctors told her it was because of the excess hormones."

Great. Not only was I super stressed out, but now I also had to worry about the pregnancy hormones making me crazy.

It wasn't like I needed the extra help. I was already so stressed between Dick being back in my life and the baby.

"Have you told him yet?" Gillian asked quietly, and I shook my head.

"I don't know if I'm going to."

She snickered. "Well, eventually, you're going to start showing and you'll have no choice."

Not if I'm out of town by then.

But could I really do that? Could I really leave Wagontown and Oliver and never tell him about the baby we made, growing in my belly? I didn't know if I could keep this up, lying to him, avoiding him.

By the time the doctor's appointment rolled around, I had barely seen Oliver in a week. I'd seen him here and there during my shifts at the bar, but I'd been sure to keep myself busy and have Gillian pick me up before close.

The doctor's office felt oddly cold, and I felt myself shiver in the cool air of the lobby.

Gillian put an arm around my shoulders, warming me up. I leaned against her, smiling gratefully.

"I don't know what I would do without you, Gilly," I said softly, and she smiled at me.

"Perish," she said matter-of-factly, and I couldn't help but laugh.

The doctor did an ultrasound after the pelvic exam, and the baby showed up immediately onscreen like a little peanut.

"You appear to be about ten weeks along," she said. That made sense. It was approximately the time I'd arrived back in Wagontown, the first night that Oliver and I had spent together.

"What about the gender?" my sister asked. The doctor smiled and shook her head.

"We won't be able to tell for another ten weeks."

"Ten weeks?" Gillian whined. "That's so far away!"

"That'll be right around the date of your next ultrasound, barring any issues," she said to me. "Do you have any questions?"

"Are pregnancy hormones a real thing?" I asked, frowning.

"Most definitely, they're a real thing," she said with a chuckle. "And you're probably experiencing them right now. You get a rush of hormones when you're in your first trimester."

"So it's technically not her fault if she acts crazy?" Gillian asked, and the doctor chuckled again.

"Not all her fault."

I had to admit that was good to hear. I'd been awful to Oliver, and I needed to apologize, but I couldn't seem to bring myself to do it. I just kept avoiding him.

"You sure you don't want me to take you back to the cabin?" Gillian asked, and I shook my head.

"I think I need to stay with you a little while longer." I smiled at her gratefully. "Thank you for helping me and taking care of me, Gilly."

"Of course," she replied, but there was a slight hesitation to her tone.

"Gilly? What's going on?"

"I heard from Mom," she said quietly, and you could

have bowled me over with a feather, for how surprised I was.

"Mom? Really? After all this time?"

"She heard you were back in Wagontown. I guess she's still got friends here," Gillian explained. "She... she wants to see you."

"You didn't tell her—"

"No, of course not!" Gillian exclaimed. "I wouldn't."

"Thank God," I breathed. I didn't know if I even wanted to see my mother, much less if I wanted to tell her that I was pregnant, and she was expecting a grandchild.

"I think it would be a good idea to talk to her," Gillian said softly.

I thought about it for a moment. Although I wasn't entirely sure I wanted to see my mother, I knew it might not be such a bad idea to try and mend fences. "Will you be there with me?"

"Of course," Gillian frowned, almost seeming offended that I'd asked.

"Then... I guess we can set something up," I said hesitantly. If I was going to have this baby, I needed all the people in my life that loved and supported me. Not just Gillian. I couldn't put everything on her, as wonderful as she was.

I took a deep breath, looking out the window as we drove back to her place.

I hoped the upcoming meeting with Mom would go better than I was expecting it too.

* * *

I assumed my mother would dote on Gillian when she

arrived and basically ignore me like always, but that wasn't what happened at all.

She rushed over to me, arms open wide, and I let her hug me tightly.

"God, it's been so long, Lex," she whispered, and when she pulled away, there were tears in her eyes.

"Yes, it has," I hedged, not sure how to react to all this attention. On one hand, I wanted to believe it was genuine, but on the other, I was wary.

"Where have you been? What have you been up to?" she asked, sitting across from me as I sat down on the recliner.

Gillian sat quietly on the couch, not speaking.

"Gosh, there's a couple of loaded questions," I breathed, and before I knew it, I was telling my mother everything. I told her about Dick, about my runaway bride episode, about Oliver, about how he was helping me and how we'd started hooking up. Finally, I told her about my pregnancy.

"You're... I'm going to be a grandmother?" she whispered, tears falling down her face.

"You are," I confirmed, allowing myself to smile. Gillian sat with her arms crossed, seeming upset.

"So why have you just now reached out, Mom? Where's Dad? What's going on?"

My mother swallowed hard. "I've left your father," she admitted.

I blinked, shocked. She'd always stood by Dad, even when he'd been super critical of me and even Gillian. He'd never been physically abusive, but words could hurt, too.

"When did this happen?" Gillian demanded to know.

"A few weeks ago." Mom went quiet for a moment before speaking again. "I heard about Lexie being back in town, and I wanted to see her. I wanted to see both of you."

"Why did you leave him?" Gillian asked.

She sighed. "There's a lot that goes on in a marriage that the kids don't know about," she admitted, and I nodded, believing that was true. "But you both know how your father is. He seemed content to never see his girls again, and I couldn't handle that. I love you both, and I'm sorry that I've been distant all these years."

It sounded almost too good to be true, and I didn't know if I could trust it.

"I'd love to throw you a baby shower. We should meet with Oliver, see how he feels about that," my mother chirped, and I went pale.

"I haven't told Oliver yet," I admitted, and my mother's blue eyes widened.

"You haven't?"

"I've been on the fence about whether or not I would be staying in Wagontown," I admitted. "I've been saving up to move away, start over."

"I can understand that, but now that you're pregnant..."

"I know," I said quickly. "You're right. I'll tell him, but... just in my own time."

"Of course, honey."

Our mother stayed for a while longer, but Gillian never came around, staying cold toward her. When Mom left, I turned to Gillian, and she narrowed her eyes.

"Something's up," she said. "Why would she leave Dad after all these years? And why does she suddenly want to see us?"

"Maybe she's just now realizing the error of her ways, Gilly. You never know."

She snorted. "Seems suspicious, that's all I'm saying."

It was surprising, sure, but suspicious? It felt as if

Gillian simply didn't trust our parents, and honestly, I could understand the feeling.

"Are you ready to go?" Gillian asked, grabbing her keys, and I cursed. I'd nearly forgotten I had a shift at the bar.

I sighed as I walked to the car, rubbing my stomach. At least I'd stopped throwing up so much in the past couple of weeks. I felt like I could keep a lot more down, and that was good news for my two jobs.

I'd only missed two shifts from each job, and I knew that wasn't much given everything that had happened. It was just that I hated ever calling out sick, for any reason. I had always been a hard and reliable worker.

Thankfully, Agnes and Oliver understood that I needed a couple of days off. This was my third shift at the bar since I took the time, and Oliver had barely surfaced the last few shifts I'd worked.

I had the feeling that he'd be around more tonight, though, because we were having a Mardi Gras-themed party, offering half-off drinks to anyone wearing beads, masks, or other Mardi Gras attire.

Gillian hugged me before she dropped me off, and I dragged myself inside to the bar, which was already hopping with activity.

I wasn't sure I was up for this much running around, but I had to be. I sipped a soda, just enough caffeine to perk me up, the carbonation always a soothing welcome for my belly. I then got started cleaning the bar and setting up.

Krista walked up behind me. "You look great tonight, Lex."

I looked down at myself then back at her sceptically. I was wearing a black pair of slacks that hid the slight pooch of my belly and a purple, button-up blouse, along with my comfortable, black ballerina flats.

"I didn't dress up much," I admitted.

She put a few beads over my head, and I smiled. "There. Now you're ready for Mardi Gras night."

"It's Fat Tuesday!" someone yelled from the crowd, and everyone else cheered, making my ears ache.

I plastered on a smile, taking drink orders and running around like a chicken with my head cut off.

Tonight was going to be a long shift.

Chapter 22

Oliver

F at Tuesday was going to be one for the books, that was for sure. We'd already cleared a hundred patrons by the time seven p.m. rolled around, and I was seeing dollar signs. I was also seeing Lexie waning, though, so I pulled Krista into my office during a rare dry spell.

"What's up, boss?"

"Keep an eye on Lex," I said, and she frowned.

"What do you mean? She's been doing great."

"I know, but she hasn't been feeling well," I mumbled. "Just... watch out for her."

Krista grinned. "You know, I heard you were sweet on her back in high school, but I didn't know you still were."

"I'm not," I argued, but Krista just shook her head, laughing, and walked back out to the bar.

Great. Now my head bartender knew how crazy I was about Lexie Tripp. Was it that obvious?

Clayton came in through the back, smiling broadly when he saw me. I greeted him with a half-hug, but he pulled me into a full one, a bearhug, really, nearly picking me up off my feet. Which wasn't easy considering I was six-foot-three.

But Clayton was a big man. Theresa was with him, wearing beads and a little flapper dress, already appearing slightly intoxicated.

"You're doing such a great job, Oliver," she said, smiling brightly at me. "The place is absolutely booming."

"I'm doing my best," I said, smiling back at her. Clayton took her by the hand and led her to the bar. I hailed Krista to tell her anything for them would be on the house. She nodded in understanding, but Clayton ended up tipping her and Lexie generously regardless.

It was nice to see Clayton out and about, having a good time. He'd always been working whenever I'd seen him before, and I'd never seen him out with his wife.

They seemed happy, and I couldn't help but feel a pang of jealousy. I'd wanted that, once upon a time. I guess I still did. And I also knew who I wanted it with—Lexie Tripp.

I knew that I'd forgiven her for what happened when we were teens, or at least I told myself I had. We were young and stupid, and maybe I'd overreacted. I'd never gotten absolute proof, although I knew my father wouldn't lie to me.

There had to be a way to find our way back to each other, even if she did want out of Wagontown. Hell, maybe I'd even go with her. All I knew was that I needed to talk to her so badly my heart ached.

She'd been avoiding me, and it hurt not to be around her even though we worked together and lived next door to each other.

I was waiting for a break in the business to talk to her, but it didn't seem to be letting up. Every time I saw Lexie, she was making a drink or talking to a customer. I was starting to get dizzy, watching her flit around, so I finally started taking drink orders for her, repeating them to Krista to put into the computer.

"Thanks," Lexie said breathlessly as she walked by, hurrying to make a tray of drinks. I helped her carry them, and within a few hours, we'd finally gotten somewhat caught up, despite the way the bar was packed to the gills.

I saw Lexie head outside for a break and decided to get some fresh air myself. I found her sitting on a crate in the alley, breathing out slow, long breaths.

"You all right?"

"Fine," she said, looking up at me with a smile. "Just tired."

"It's already been a long night."

She groaned. "And it's not even close to over."

"We're going to make it through," I promised her. She stood, smiling softly up at me.

God, I wanted to kiss her. I wanted to kiss the trail of freckles along her nose, down her jawline, her neck.

"Lexie," I whispered. She tilted her head up slightly and I took the opportunity to kiss her, leaning down, pressing my mouth to hers.

Lexie relaxed against me, her hands going to my chest, but she didn't push me away, making my heart soar.

"Boss!" Krista called, her eyes widening when she caught me and Lexie making out in the alley. "Oops. Sorry to interrupt, but I need another few bottles of Tito's for this party."

I hurried inside, my face flushed, to crack open the liquor cabinet and get her what she needed. I couldn't believe I'd let Krista catch us. I was definitely going to have to explain to her that she couldn't say a word about it.

But why couldn't she? Didn't I want the whole world to

know? I wanted Lexie Tripp to be mine, and I wasn't ashamed of that. Not anymore.

I missed Lexie coming back inside, losing track of her for another hour while we were all busy working. I was busy helping Krista pour drinks when I finally caught sight of Lexie, her head thrown back, laughing at something a customer had said.

It wasn't until I got closer that I recognized the customer—Tristan.

My blood turned to ice in my veins. It was later in the night, and everyone seemed to be in the process of leaving, but not Tristan. She had her hand on his arm, and it suddenly felt like I was back in time, back to when my father told me that Lexie and Tristan had something going on.

My blood had run cold then, too.

"What are you talking about?" I asked, my voice cracking.

"Don't you think they spend too much time together?"

"They're friends," I said, defending them, but my father looked me right in the eye.

"I caught them," he said. "Kissing out on the terrace on the fourth of July."

"No," I breathed. "You didn't. She wouldn't."

My father shrugged. "I just can't stand seeing my son being a pushover in my own house."

My breath had become short and I'd taken off, looking for Tristan and Lexie.

That was it. That was the moment that had ruined all my hopes and dreams for any future with Lexie.

I didn't think, I just stalked across the bar and grabbed Tristan's arm, yanking him away from her.

"Oliver," he said quietly. "We were just talking."

That was exactly what he'd said that day years ago.

"Just talking, huh? Talking about what? About how you betrayed me?"

"Stop it!" Lexie nearly screamed, and Tristan and I both looked over at her, shocked. "Stop it, Oliver. I don't need to be stressed like this." She paused, breathing hard. "I'm pregnant. It's bad for the baby."

It's bad for the *what?*

Chapter 23

Lexie

Oliver grabbed my arm, dragging me into the back office. I sighed heavily. I hadn't wanted to tell him this way. I wanted to wait until after my shift was over, after all the business was concluded. I wanted to tell him at home, where we could talk about things in complete privacy, where it wouldn't be so stressful.

But he'd freaked out about Tristan—again—and I'd just blurted it out. I couldn't help myself. I was already so stressed out, and the only way that I could convince him to leave Tristan alone was to tell him the truth.

"What the hell did you just say?" Oliver asked in a low voice.

"I'm pregnant."

"And it's—"

"Of course it's yours," I snapped. "Who else would it be?"

Don't you dare say Tristan. Oliver clenched his jaw shut, not saying anything for a long moment.

"Why didn't you tell me before now?"

179

"I don't know," I said miserably. "I've been trying to wrap my head around it."

He sighed. "And you're sure it's mine?"

"Oliver, if you ask me that one more time—"

"Sorry, sorry," he apologized quickly, his brows drawing together in a frown. "It's just a lot to process, especially with the way you just sprung it on me."

"I know it is," I said calmly. "And I'm sorry about that. But can't you see why I didn't tell you before now? If you still can't trust me around Tristan, why should I think you'll trust me to be a good mother?"

"How am I supposed to trust you around Tristan?" he snapped, anger flashing in his brown eyes.

"You're supposed to trust me *period*, Oliver. But you don't and you never have." I was angry, but I was more tired than angry. Tired of Oliver not trusting me, tired of him always believing that I was sneaking around behind his back.

"We aren't even together," Oliver argued. "Why would I trust you when—"

"Because it's *me*, Ollie," I said passionately, pointing at my chest. "Because you didn't believe me then and you should have. Just as you should believe me now. I only ever wanted you."

Oliver went quiet for a long moment, too long.

"I was thrown into fatherhood unexpectedly with Trent because of how his mother handled things," he said quietly. "I don't want to miss out on this baby's life. That being said, we can be civil and co-parent. We can be friends."

I stared at him incredulously. "Is that what you want? To be... *friends*?" I almost spat the word out.

"Isn't that what you want? You broke things off, Lex. Don't act like—"

"Act like what? Like I care? I *do* care, Oliver. That's why...." I took in a deep breath, stopping myself before I said something I'd regret. Talking was clearly getting us nowhere. "I need to finish cleaning up."

I started to head out of the office, but Oliver grabbed my hand before I reached the door, pulling me back toward him.

"I don't see any other way, Lex," he said, his voice sounding almost pained. "I wasn't able to trust you back then, and you're right, I can't trust you now. I thought... I thought I was over it, but seeing you with him..."

"I wasn't with him," I said through gritted teeth, yanking my hand away. "I was just talking to him. Just like all those years ago, Oliver. You were wrong then, and you're wrong now."

Oliver looked at me for a brief moment before averting his gaze. "I want to go to doctor's appointments. I want to be there throughout the pregnancy."

"Fine," I said tightly. "You can be at doctor's appointments. You can see the baby whenever you want." I paused. "But I'm leaving Wagontown as soon as the baby's born and settled. I'm starting a new life. You can travel to see your child."

His eyes shot back to mine, but he didn't protest, his mouth twisting in a sort of snarl.

"I'm sorry, Lexie. But I'm always going to be suspicious of you and Tristan. I just can't forgive you."

"There's nothing to forgive and there never has been," I barked, before walking out of the office and hurrying back to the bar to help clean up.

"Are you all right?" Krista asked in a low voice, her eyes wide. I only nodded, sweeping furiously, allowing my anger to guide the broom.

By the time I was done, all of the customers were gone except for Tristan, who stood near the back door.

I walked up to him, putting my hand on his arm to get his attention.

He turned to look at me, a sheepish smile on his face.

"I didn't mean to cause drama, Lex, I really didn't."

"I know you didn't," I said easily. "But listen, I could use a ride home, if you're able."

"Of course," he replied, surprise evident on his handsome face.

I could feel Oliver's eyes on us as we left the Pig, but I didn't care. Let him be mad. He'd never given me the benefit of the doubt, never trusted me, and I was right that he'd never trust me now.

We couldn't be together. Not ever, not if he couldn't put any faith in me.

"I wish I knew where Oliver got the idea that we were hooking up," Tristan said after we were on the road.

I huffed out a breath. "Me, too. He's crazy about it. He always has been."

"He's still crazy about you," Tristan said softly.

I snorted. "He sure has a funny way of showing it."

"He wouldn't still be jealous if he didn't care, Lex. He'd be over it by now."

"It doesn't matter if he cares or not," I said firmly. "He admitted he can't trust me. A relationship is nothing without trust."

"And what about the baby?" he asked, then winced slightly. "Sorry. I know that's none of my business."

I smiled at him. "We're friends," I said. "Of course it's your business. Not to mention I blurted it out right in front of you."

"I have to admit I was surprised," he chuckled.

I smiled at him. Tristan had always been a good friend to me, and to Oliver, but it'd been years since I'd allowed myself to think about him. Oliver had messed me up so much by not trusting me, accusing me of sleeping with his best friend behind his back.

Oliver had never been the jealous type, and I had no idea where he'd gotten the idea that Tristan and I were sleeping together back then.

"He'll always be in the baby's life. We'll be civil, we just can't be together," I stated, and Tristan nodded.

After giving him directions, he showed no surprise that I was living in Oliver's cabin, but I was sure he was curious. I was grateful he didn't ask more questions, though.

I only wanted to go there to pack up my things. I planned on moving in with Gillian after tonight, not wanting to be around Oliver all the time. I knew it would drive me crazy.

Tristan smiled and waved at me as I got out of the car. "Don't be a stranger," he said, and I smiled back.

"I won't. No reason to be."

I closed the car door softly then went inside, packing a few essentials before calling Gillian.

"Pick me up at the cabin," I said after she answered.

"Lex?" She sounded concerned.

"I'll explain on the way home," I promised.

"Be there soon."

I packed a few more things as I waited, telling myself I'd get the rest later. I had a shift at the store in the morning, and I wanted to get a few hours of decent sleep. Not that I really believed I could. Spending the night away from Oliver, away from the cabin would do me some good.

Tears began to burn at the backs of my eyes as I waited

on the porch for Gillian, and I all but jumped into her car before she put it in park.

"Oh, Lex. What happened?" she asked, and I burst into tears.

"Just drive," I sobbed, and she did. I didn't want to see Oliver tearing into the driveway, mad and jealous for no reason over Tristan.

I'd never done anything to hurt him, and it just about killed me that he thought I would. I had no idea how he'd gotten that idea back then, or even now, but I guessed it didn't matter anymore.

Love meant trust, and if he couldn't trust me...

"I told him about the baby," I muttered. "And he just wants to be friends."

Gillian gasped. "Friends? He really said that? Oh my God, men are such assholes."

"Yeah, well, it doesn't matter now," I said, wiping at my face. "I've got a baby to worry about, regardless of what he wants our relationship to be."

I started to sob again. Gillian steered the car over to the shoulder of the road and took me into her arms.

"I'll be there for you. Maybe Mom will too. I know she can be flaky, but maybe she means it this time," she said, rubbing my back to comfort me.

After I managed to get myself together, Gillian pulled back onto the highway. We made it home without further incident, and I tiredly dragged my stuff inside, planting it in her guest room.

"Are you going to be okay tonight?" Gillian asked quietly.

"Would you sleep in my bed with me?" I asked in a small voice. "Just for tonight?"

"Of course," she said, climbing into bed with me after

washing our faces, brushing our teeth, and putting our jammies on.

I laid in bed next to my baby sister for the first time since we were kids, looking up at the ceiling and wondering if I'd ever get to sleep.

Oliver didn't love me. He couldn't, not after the way he'd acted tonight. I'd hoped the baby would change things. I thought Oliver had gotten past his feelings from years ago, that I could forgive him for being young and jealous.

But he was the same person now as he was then, despite being an excellent father.

I guess that was the one thing I could count on.

We'd never be together, but I knew he'd be good to our child.

It was the best I could hope for.

Chapter 24

Oliver

It made me feel completely crazy, jealous, and full of rage seeing Lexie leave with Tristan. I wanted to rush after them, run them down, pull Tristan out of the car and punch him over and over.

But on the other hand, I'd been a complete ass to Lexie, especially after she'd revealed she was pregnant. How many times had I asked her if the baby was mine?

I didn't know what to do. I'd lied to Lexie when I said I just wanted to be friends. I wanted more, so much more. I wanted all of her. And I wanted this baby, too. But I'd been too damn stupid and jealous to admit it.

She was right, I didn't trust her. I hadn't trusted her back then when she told me she'd never cheated on me, and I didn't trust her now. I didn't know if I ever could. The fact that she wouldn't own up to it, even years later, made me nuts.

Tristan had always denied it as well. So I couldn't help but wonder, was it really true? Had I been wrong all this time?

I went straight home without picking Trent up from my mom's. I needed some time to think. I also needed a drink, and I didn't like to drink around Trent, even if he was sleeping. I swallowed hard as I drove past Lexie's cabin and noticed all the lights were off. She was either not there, which made my heart seize in my chest, or she'd gone right to bed.

If she wasn't there, was she with Tristan?

I immediately pushed that thought out of my head. I had to think, *really* think. I couldn't risk coloring my thoughts with anger and jealousy and that's exactly what would happen if I thought about Tristan.

He'd been my best friend since we were in middle school, and the betrayal was almost as bad as breaking up with Lexie. It was a double whammy, and it felt like I'd lost everything all at once.

But my father had told me he'd seen them kissing. He'd *seen* them. What reason would he have to lie to me about that? He knew it would cut me to the core. Sure, he'd never really liked Lexie, or Tristan for that matter. He'd said they were beneath me, that both of them were from what he considered "the wrong side of the tracks," but he'd only wanted me to be happy.

He had known how happy Lexie made me. He'd also known that Tristan was my best friend.

Hadn't he?

Maybe I needed to talk to him. God knew I needed to talk to *someone*. Instead of drinking myself into a stupor, I called him. It was late, after midnight, but he picked up right away.

"What are you doing awake?" I asked him when he answered.

"Don't sleep much these days," he admitted.

187

I wanted to say I was sorry to hear that, but in that moment I was glad he was up.

"I need to talk to you, Dad. Can I come over?"

"Always, son. Is everything okay?"

I paused. "Not really," I confessed.

"Oliver—"

"I'll be there soon," I said, cutting him off. I didn't want to have this conversation over the phone.

I broke all manner of traffic laws getting to my father's place. He was standing on the porch, smoking a cigar, when I arrived.

"I thought you stopped smoking," I said as I walked up the steps.

He sighed. "I only have one a week."

"Still. It's bad for you."

"Don't I know it," he chuckled, looking at me. There was something in his eyes I couldn't quite name. "What's going on, son?"

"Do you remember when you told me that Tristan and Lexie were seeing each other behind my back? That you had witnessed them kissing?" I asked, cutting to the chase.

"Of course I do," he muttered, sitting down on the rocking chair. I sat perched on the porch railing across from him.

"You said you saw them, right?"

"Oliver..."

"Dad, you have to make me understand," I said, my voice breaking. "Because I'm going crazy. You saw them, right? Kissing? On the terrace?"

"Listen, son. Lexie, she wasn't the right girl for you. Or at least I didn't think so, back then."

"She wasn't the right girl because she was unfaithful," I said flatly, but my father wouldn't look at me. "Right, Dad?"

"I didn't see them," he said finally. My eyes widened so big I wondered if they'd bulge out of their sockets.

"You *what*?"

"I didn't see them, son. I just... I suspected it." He spread his hands wide, in a defensive manner. If he wasn't my father, I think I would have hit him.

"You suspected it? You blew up my whole life based on suspicion?"

"Girls that age aren't known for their loyalty," he said, clearing his throat, trying to defend himself. "And you were so blindly in love, Ollie. You thought you were going to marry her."

"I would have married her," I said fiercely, gritting my teeth. "I would have married her, but you ruined that! How could you do that to me?"

My father leaned forward and put his head in his hands. "I'm so sorry," he choked out. "Your mother and I, we've been fighting about this ever since it happened. She suspected that I lied, and she told me I was playing God with your life, but Oliver, I just wanted to protect you."

"Protect me from what? Marrying the love of my life?"

"It would have been a mistake," he said firmly. "She wasn't right for you. You were too young. It wouldn't have worked out."

I stood up, pacing around in a circle to try and keep myself sane. "That wasn't your decision to make! You should have never lied to me. Not only did you ruin my relationship with Lexie, but you also destroyed my friendship with Tristan!" I breathed in deeply. "As a matter of fact, you're still ruining it. You've lied to me all these years, and for what?"

"She wasn't good enough for you!" my father burst out, and I stared at him, unblinking.

"Why, because she didn't come from money? Because her parents didn't give her a trust fund?"

"It's not like that, son. You know I worked for everything I had—"

"Sure, with help from a loan from your daddy to get started," I snarled. "You always had what you needed growing up. I'm not saying you didn't work hard—you did, and so did I—but we always had help along the way and plenty of support."

"Lexie didn't have that and neither did Tristan," my father said. "They would have only brought you down with them."

"You *broke* my *heart*," I said, tears burning at the backs of my eyes. "You ruined everything. How am I ever supposed to forgive you?"

"It was years ago," he said shakily. "You don't have to dwell on it, Oliver—"

"She's pregnant. With my baby. Your grandchild."

He gasped. "You can't be serious."

"I'm dead serious. All this time, we could have been together, and now you might have ruined everything forever."

"I didn't realize what I was doing," he backtracked. "I didn't realize what heartbreak was, not until your mother left me." He paused. "I'm sorry, Ollie. I'm so sorry."

"You should be," I hissed. "Because I don't know if I can ever forgive you or if I'll ever even talk to you again."

My head was spinning and I didn't know which way was up. I managed to make it back to my car and headed straight to my mother's place.

She'd left my father because of this fight. She'd been on my side.

When she opened the door, blinking sleep out of her eyes, she didn't say a word, just pulled me into her arms.

I pressed my face against her neck, breaking down, and she held me, patting my back.

"Oh, Oliver, I'm so sorry," she murmured. I knew that she knew that Dad had come clean.

After a few moments, I got myself together, and once again we sat down at the kitchen table with a pot of tea.

"Your father didn't understand young love. He and I met when we were older, and he didn't get it."

"And you did?" I asked, curious.

She smiled. "Your father wasn't my first love, Ollie. I, too, had a high school sweetheart I was crazy about. But he went off to college and broke my heart. Your father never understood how that felt."

"Not until now," I said quietly. My mother's eyes widened. "He said he understands, now that you've left him."

"It wasn't just the lie that made me leave him," Mom pointed out. "You know that, right?"

I nodded. "I know that, Mom."

"So it's not your fault, Oliver. Don't ever think that, okay?"

I nodded again, feeling empty and hollow, my heart aching.

"I should have trusted her," I said softly. "And now, I don't know if she will ever forgive me."

"Of course she will. She's the love of your life, isn't she?"

"God help me, yes, she is. And she's carrying my baby."

"Oh, Ollie," my mother whispered, tears streaming down her face. "I'm so happy for you. I know how you've always felt about Lexie, and I know this is what you want."

"I want it so much," I admitted. "But now I'm afraid she'll never talk to me again."

"Of course she will, honey. She still loves you just as much as you love her."

"I don't know about that," I said miserably. "Not after how I acted tonight." I sighed. "Tristan showed up at the bar."

My mother frowned. "You made an ass of yourself, didn't you?"

"Yeah, I did," I groaned. "I was just so angry, so jealous."

"But you wouldn't be so angry if you didn't still care about her. You still love her, don't you?"

"Yes, so much." I rubbed a hand across my face. "What do I do?"

"You talk to her," she said simply, making it sound easy. "You go to her and apologize, tell her you know what an ass you've been, and hope that she forgives you."

"What if—"

"No what ifs, son. It might take some time. She might need some space. But if it's meant to be, she'll come back to you." She smiled. "And you'd better take care of that new grandbaby of mine."

"Of course I will."

"Do you want to crash on the pull-out again?" she asked, and I nodded, giving her a grateful half-smile.

The pull-out had almost become a more comfortable space than my own bed, with my mother's comforting vibe everywhere around me. I thought about Trent, how I had to tell him that he'd be a big brother soon. I thought about Lexie, hoping against hope that she would forgive me.

I even thought about Tristan, wondering if I could ever get his friendship back.

All I could do was try.

Chapter 25

Lexie

I woke up at Gillian's to my phone buzzing, and when I looked at it, I saw that I had three missed calls from Oliver and several text messages.

Please talk to me.

Lex, I'm sorry. I need to talk to you.

Lex, I love you.

That last one made me bolt upright in bed. Gillian groaned, sitting up and wiping at her eyes.

"You're up early," she commented. "Thought you only had the bar shift tonight."

"Oliver texted me," I said, showing her the phone screen.

Her eyes widened. "He loves you? Wow."

"Right?" I huffed. I was still angry, and I didn't know if I wanted to talk to him. But I couldn't help my heart from soaring after seeing that message. Did he mean it?

After how he'd acted after seeing me and Tristan, I couldn't imagine that he would even want to talk to me, much less be declaring his love for me.

I got up and headed for the shower, trying to push

Oliver out of my mind, but that message kept coming back, floating in my memory.

Lex, I love you.

God, if only that were true. It would mean the world. But it wouldn't mean that I forgave him. I took in a deep breath, letting the water wash away my stress and worries. He was the one who said we should just be friends. He was the one that went after Tristan because he didn't trust me.

I never did anything wrong. I never cheated on him. I loved him with everything in me, and he just threw it away. I lost Tristan and Oliver in one fell swoop, Tristan had been my close friend too. I'd lost all my hopes and dreams because Oliver thought I was cheating when I wasn't.

My phone buzzed on my nightstand as soon as I started to get dressed and I groaned, walking toward it. It was Krista.

I picked it up, my hair still dripping. "Hello?"

"Thank God you answered," she breathed. "I really need your help."

"My help?"

"Someone just called in to reserve the entire place. There's going to be close to two hundred people. We'll be at capacity. I called Raoul, but we still need another server." She sighed. "Another three servers and bartenders, really, but we only have what we have."

My eyes widened. "Holy cow. Okay, I can come in. What time?"

She paused. "In an hour."

I gasped. "An hour?"

"Oliver said he'll come in to help too."

Suddenly, I wasn't so sure I could make it. "I don't know, Krista, that's really short notice."

"Please, Lex. We really need you. You'll make a lot of

money, at least five hundred in tips. I've waited on these people before and they're big tippers," she pleaded.

I drew in a breath. Five hundred dollars for a shift was something I wasn't in the position to turn down. Especially with the baby coming.

I sighed. "All right. I'll be there."

"Thank you, thank you, thank you," she chanted. "See you soon."

She hung up and I hurried to get dressed, towel-drying my hair, and letting it lie damp. It would be a little extra curly, but I planned on putting it up in a ponytail later anyway.

I put on some light makeup and a pair of jeans that were starting to get a little too tight, and a simple V-neck shirt.

Oliver generally didn't care what we wore, and I thought the outfit made me look pretty good.

"Where are you off to?" Gillian asked as I went into the living room, grabbing my purse.

"Work," I said quickly. "The Pig got rented out by some big wigs and they need me there early. Can you give me a ride?"

She whistles. "Of course. I hope you make good money, but don't you think you should consider giving up one of your jobs? I mean, the baby..."

"I'll be fine," I assured her. "Women work through their pregnancies all the time. Plus, it's still early."

"Okay," she said slowly as she got out of bed. "I just worry about you."

I smiled at her, feeling a wave of affection for my baby sister. The one great thing about coming back to Wagontown was reconnecting with her.

After throwing on a pair of sweats and a t-shirt, Gilly grabbed her keys. "Let's go," she said with a grin.

When we arrived at the Pig, I turned to my sister. "Thanks, Gilly, for everything. I'll see you later."

She waved and smiled and I got out of the car, anxiously hurrying inside. I had no idea what this shift would bring.

It still seemed kind of strange that the place belonged to Oliver now; all the work he'd done had given it a different feel. It wasn't bad, but I missed the old Pig every once in a while. After all, it held a lot of nostalgia for me.

As soon as I walked in the door, I spotted Krista cutting up lemons and limes at warp speed.

She hissed and put her finger in her mouth. "Stupid citrus acid," she grumbled.

"You shouldn't bite your cuticles," I scolded, knowing it was a bad habit of hers. I put my hair up and washed my hands, nudging her aside with my hip and taking over.

Her finger still in her mouth, Krista wrinkled her nose, turning to wash her hands and get the rest of the bar ready. She pulled down the top shelf liquor—expensive vodkas, tequilas, rums, and bourbons.

My eyes widened. "They really must be good tippers, ordering everything top shelf."

"They really are," she chuckled. "They're a little needy, but they're very nice and very rich."

"Is it a business or something?" I asked, curious. I didn't know that many rich people in Wagontown other than Oliver and his family.

She nodded. "It's Oliver's board."

I froze. "So it's the people he works with?"

"Everyone on the oil magnate board." She paused. "I think his dad is coming, too."

I let out a long breath. *Great.* "Perfect," I mumbled, and Krista raised an eyebrow but didn't push.

There was too much to do for her to be nosy, I guess.

It took us about half an hour to get everything set up, and by then, people were already starting to trickle in. There were men in three-piece suits that probably cost more than my car, the women wearing expensive shoes and toting designer handbags.

They started to sit down as I finished setting up the bar, Krista and Raoul taking orders. We'd decided that since I was the fastest pourer, I'd stay behind the bar until they began to order entrees. I bounced on my heels, waiting for the orders, and when they started to come in, I began to pour. I was sweating by the time I finished the first round, grateful that Raoul and Krista were serving.

I huffed out a breath and walked back to the walk-in freezer to get some cool air. It helped a lot, especially since I was starting to feel dizzy. Maybe Gillian was right. Maybe I should think about lowering my hours. I certainly wanted to keep the baby safe. I was starting to show, but the apron covered it.

I hurried back out to the bar, seeing that I had a couple more drink orders. While I was making them, Oliver's father walked in.

I lowered my head and focused on the drinks, trying to avoid eye contact, but he walked right up to the bar anyway.

"Alexandra?" he called softly.

I hated it when people called me by my full name. It always made me feel like I was in trouble or something, because my parents only did it when I was being scolded.

"Lexie," I corrected him, looking up into his eyes, so much like Oliver's.

He was a handsome man and he was aging well, even if his belly was a little rounded. Oliver clearly got the best from both of them.

"Lexie. It's lovely to see you."

"Is it?" I asked dryly.

He leaned forward, lowering his tone. "Oliver told me about my grandchild. I just wanted to say congratulations." He paused. "And that... I'm sorry."

I tilted my head. "Sorry for what?"

He sighed. "I know I was awful to you back then. I know that I messed things up between you and Oliver."

"What do you mean?" Confusion rushed over me, threatening to turn into panic. "How did you ruin things?"

"By telling him to suspect you and Tristan," he answered, looking down as if ashamed.

"It was you?" I gasped.

No wonder Oliver hadn't believed me. His own father told him that I was some kind of floozy.

"I'm sorry, Lexie," he said. "I hope one day you can forgive me."

He walked away, toward one of the tables, and all I could do was stare straight ahead, shell-shocked.

I always knew that his father didn't like me, but I never thought he'd sabotage our relationship. I understood better now why Oliver believed something had happened, but he should have trusted me. He should have believed in our love.

I cleared my throat as more orders came through on the printer, throwing myself into work, steadily making the drinks and keeping the ice cooler full. I was glad I didn't have to speak to anyone other than Krista and Raoul. My head was spinning, and I didn't think I'd be very good company to patrons.

"Are you all right?" Raoul asked softly as he came over to get a couple of rum and cokes.

I wiped sweat from my brow. "Sure. Just tired."

"We could switch places, if you'd like," he offered, and I smiled at him gratefully.

"Thanks, but I'd rather stay behind the bar. I'm not used to dealing with all these rich folks."

He chuckled. "Me, either. But it'll be worth it when we split our tips."

I nodded and he took off with the drinks. Oliver was nowhere in sight, and I was surprised. He'd said that he'd be there to help.

It was another hour before he showed up, coming through the door looking disheveled and flustered.

"Sorry I'm late," he muttered to Krista.

"It's okay," she said. "Please help Lexie behind the bar."

I winced and groaned inwardly. We were going to be in close proximity, pouring drinks together, but what could I do? Refuse? He was my boss.

Oliver came behind the bar and I was surprised he didn't smell like whiskey. I'd been sure he'd been drinking last night when he sent those text messages.

"Everything okay?" I asked quietly, a little worried.

"Trent has a high fever," he answered, filling cups with ice to help the orders move along quicker. "He's with his grandmother."

I frowned. "Poor guy. I hope he feels better soon."

Oliver turned to me, his eyes intense, and I couldn't help but turn away. When he looked at me like that, it made my knees weak, and I was determined to still be angry with him.

I'd lost everything when he broke up with me, moving out of Wagontown to recover.

I continued to focus on pouring drinks as they came in, avoiding Oliver as much as possible. We worked in silence but we were a good team, making sure that each drink was perfect.

When I went to each table and booth to bus drink glasses since we were running low, Oliver's father stared at me. I didn't know what he expected. Did he want me to forgive him after everything his lies caused?

I knew he was my child's grandfather, and I wouldn't keep them apart, but as for a relationship with me, that wasn't going to happen.

It was nearly dusk by the time everyone trailed out. Krista, Raoul, and I were counting our tips at a back table when Oliver walked over.

"Don't tell me we're opening up to the public," Krista groaned.

Oliver scoffed. "Hell, no. We've had a long day. Our regulars can wait until tomorrow night to come and drink."

"Thank God," Raoul breathed, and I laughed a little.

We'd made almost six-hundred dollars each, and I was over the moon. It was going right into my savings so that eventually, I could start a new life anywhere but here.

"Lexie, can I talk to you?" Oliver asked as I started to get ready to leave.

"Not tonight," I said firmly. "Gotta get home."

"Lex, please—"

Luckily, I had already called Gillian to come and pick me up, so she was waiting when I walked outside. I'd left, not even giving Oliver a second glance. I wasn't ready to talk to him. I wasn't ready to forgive him.

And I knew that looking into his soulful eyes, hearing his words, I would cave.

Chapter 26

Oliver

I couldn't help but feel depressed over the situation with Lexie.

How could I tell her how I felt, how sorry I was, if she wouldn't talk to me? I moped around the house for the next week, only leaving to go and check in on Lexie during her shifts at the Pig.

I pretended to be helping out behind the bar, or back in the office doing paperwork, but in reality, I was just watching her. I paid attention to the way she moved, to see if she was getting too tired. I was worried about her and the baby.

Not to mention, I was madly in love with her and needed her desperately.

"Daddy, why are you sad?" Trent asked me when I came in from work and got him settled for dinner.

He looked up at me with wide eyes as he ate his chicken nuggets.

"I'm not..." I started, but then I realized he clearly was picking up on my mood, and I needed to be honest with him. I'd always taught Trent not to be like me, not to push

201

down his emotions until he blew up. It was a flaw in myself I'd always disliked. "Actually, I am a little sad," I admitted.

"Why?"

"Because I lost a friend."

"Where did they go?" he asked incredulously, and I couldn't help but bark out a surprised laugh.

"Well, they didn't actually go anywhere, they just don't want to be my friend anymore."

"That is sad," he said glumly. "Maybe you can make up with them? When me and Aiden aren't friends anymore, I just say I'm sorry. And then we're friends again."

Aiden was his best friend from summer camp who he kept in close contact with.

I smiled, ruffling Trent's hair. "I'm going to try that. Thank you for the advice, kiddo."

Trent grinned. "You're welcome."

I hesitated. Was it the right time to tell him about his new little brother or sister? I decided it was. It would cheer him up, at least.

"I have some news for you, Trent."

"News?" he looked up at me blankly.

"You're going to have a little brother or sister," I told him quietly, and Trent's eyes widened.

"I am?" he gasped, bouncing in his seat.

"You are."

"Does that mean I get a new mommy, too?" he asked hopefully, and my heart clenched in my chest.

"I don't know about that, buddy," I replied gently. "But you are going to have a little playmate in a few months."

"I hope it's a boy," he said excitedly. "We're gonna be best friends."

"You can still be best friends, even if it's a girl," I assured him.

He grinned up at me. "I'm so excited!"

"I know you are," I chuckled. For the next half an hour, he babbled about all the fun things he was going to do with his sibling. It made my heart soar to know how thrilled he was about it.

He was still talking about becoming a big brother when I put him to bed, and I couldn't stop smiling. I was glad I told him; it raised my mood a lot.

I continued to text Lexie, asking her to speak to me, but she kept ignoring me. If I wasn't a single father, I might have thrown myself into a bottle the way I did after we broke up the first time, but I had responsibilities now.

I knew what I needed to do next, but it was a hard pill to swallow.

I needed to talk to Tristan. To apologize to him. I'd hurt Lexie and myself by my actions back then, but I'd also hurt my best friend, a man who'd always been there for me. He didn't deserve what happened.

The next morning, after I dropped Trent off at school, I looked in my files and found Tristan's number. I took in a deep breath and dialed.

"Hello?" he answered after a few rings. I was relieved. I knew my number had probably shown up as unknown.

"Trent, it's Oliver." There was nothing but silence, and for a moment, I thought he'd hung up.

"You've got some nerve—" he started, but I cut him off.

"Tristan, please. Just hear me out. Can we get a drink or something?"

He went quiet again. "Are you serious right now? You tried to kick my ass, more than once."

"I know," I sighed. "But I really need to talk to you. I want to apologize. Please."

"The only reason I'm entertaining this is because you were my best friend for years," he warned.

"Fair enough. Meet me at the new Irish pub downtown?"

"O'Malley's?"

"That's the one."

"See you there," he grunted, and hung up the phone.

I let out the breath I'd been holding. At least I would get a chance to apologize.

When I arrived at O'Malley's, Tristan was already there, sitting in a back booth. I slid into the seat across from him and let out a long breath.

"I should clock you one, you know."

I winced. "Do it, if it'll make you feel better."

"It won't," he said flatly.

"Tristan, I'm sorry," I said mournfully. "I know now that you never laid a hand on Lex."

"You should have known it then," he snapped, and I quickly nodded in agreement.

"You're right. I should have. I fucked up. Badly. But I'm asking you, as my old best friend, to forgive me."

He glared at me. "And why should I?"

"Because I need you," I said quietly. "I don't know which way is up. Lex is pregnant and I'm in love with her, but she won't talk to me."

"So you wanted to apologize so that you'd have someone to talk to?" he asked, but he was smiling.

"That's not the only reason, but..." I trailed off, and Tristan laughed.

"All right, Ollie, you moron. We can be friends again."

"Thank God," I groaned, banging my head against the table as the server walked over with a raised eyebrow.

Tristan snickered and ordered a pitcher of light beer.

"She isn't as forgiving as I am, I take it?" he asked, pouring us each a glass when the server returned.

"Not even a little," I admitted, taking a slow sip.

"You can't exactly blame her," he pointed out.

"I know," I sighed. "But all I want is a few moments to explain things to her."

Tristan narrowed his eyes. "Explain things to me, Ollie. What happened back then? Why were you so sure that we were fooling around behind your back?"

"My father," I said flatly. "He told me that he saw you two together. Kissing."

Tristan's blue eyes widened. "There's no way."

"He didn't, obviously. He admitted he lied about it. He said he was suspicious of how much time you two spent together." I sighed heavily. "And I guess I was too. I wasn't the jealous type before, but I couldn't stop thinking about it after he told me, and I suppose that's what made me become that way."

"You should have trusted us, Ollie. We were just friends. You, me, Lex... we were like the Three Musketeers."

"I know that now," I told him. "But at the time, I was young and jealous and stupid. And I don't know how to explain that to Lexie."

"Grovel," he said, taking another sip of beer, and I stared at him blankly.

"What?"

"You have to grovel," he told me. "You've got to throw yourself at her feet and beg her forgiveness. You've got to let go of your pride and just... grovel. Elena makes me do it all the time." He grinned. "Sometimes all that groveling turns into something more fun, too."

I blinked. "I don't know if I can do that," I admitted. I

thought I'd do anything to get Lexie back, but at the same time, showing that kind of emotion outwardly was hard for me. I usually just pushed everything down.

"Lex is a great girl. If you don't do any and everything to get her back, you're an idiot," he said, frowning.

"You're right. But how do I grovel when she won't talk to me?"

"Not sure, but I'm guessing you'll need to convince her to meet you somewhere. Maybe tell her that she left something important behind at the cabin then suggest she meet you there so you can return it to her."

"That might actually work. That's a good idea."

"Of course it is," he replied smugly. I chuckled in return.

"Enough about me. Tell me about your love life."

Tristan groaned. "Absolutely not."

"Absolutely not because it's so kinky?" I teased.

"Oh it's kinky enough, I guess," he admitted. "Working on the offshore rigs as much as I do keeps me busy. I don't have much time for romance, but Elena puts up with me."

"The Tristan I knew had a new girl on his arm every week," I said, surprised that he was sticking with dating just one woman.

"Well, that Tristan grew up."

I nodded. "I get it. I feel like I'm a totally different person from who I was back then."

"Hopefully you are. But attacking me at the Pig told me that guy is still in there somewhere."

I laughed nervously. "I'm really sorry about that."

Tristan shrugged. "We all make mistakes, old friend."

We finished the pitcher and by the time we left, I was tipsy enough that I had to call an Uber. We had parted on good terms and it felt good.

My best friend was back. Now if only I could get Lex back, too.

I looked toward the cabin as soon as I got home. The lights were all off. I sighed heavily; a part of me was hoping she would be there, but I doubted it. She must be staying with her sister. I couldn't just show up there and grovel but ultimately if I had to, I would.

Tristan was right. I had to do everything in my power to get her back.

Chapter 27

Lexie

I 'd been avoiding Oliver like the plague since our last fight. I knew I couldn't avoid him forever, though, so when he texted me asking to meet him at the cabin, I obliged. I was a bit surprised, however, when Gillian dropped me off and Oliver was sitting on the steps, looking disheveled.

"Oliver?" I walked up to him. "What are you doing?"

"I've been here all night," he said hoarsely. "I need to talk to you, Lex. Please."

His eyes were so big and hopeful, so exhausted and desperate, I couldn't deny him.

"All right," I said softly, walking up the steps and unlocking the door. Oliver followed me inside, sighing in what sounded like relief.

"Lex, I'm so sorry," he said mournfully, and I swallowed hard.

"Sorry? Is that all you have to say to me?"

"My father—" he started, but I cut him off.

"Your father told me that he was the one who told you

that I was seeing Tristan. That doesn't matter, Oliver. You never should have believed it."

"He's my father. I thought he knew what was best for me," he insisted. "I... I was stupid and jealous and I'm sorry. I can't tell you how sorry I am."

I crossed my arms over my chest. "What do you want from me, Oliver? Forgiveness? So that we can be friends?"

"I don't want to be friends," he said in a low tone, stepping closer to me. I didn't move away even though my brain was screaming at me to do just that. "You're family, Lex. You always have been."

"You're the one that said you wanted to be friends, remember?" I retort, trying to keep my tone cold but having a hard time doing it.

"It was a stupid thing to say," he said simply, and I snorted out a laugh. "I was acting jealous and not thinking clearly, the same way I was back then, but it's only because I love you so much, Lex."

I froze. That was exactly what Dick would say when he criticized my weight or my clothes or the way I did things. *It's just because I love you so much, Alexandra.*

"I can't do this," I said as I stepped away from Oliver. "I need you to leave."

"Lex," he pleaded, but I'd made up my mind, my heart aching.

"We can be civil," I continued. "We can co-parent, but we're not friends, Oliver. We never were. And we aren't anything else, either."

"Please." His words were soft, his brown eyes wide and filling with tears. My heart clenched in my chest, but I opened the door and ushered him out.

He kept staring at me from the doorway, and finally, I shut the door in his face.

I leaned against it, sliding down to the floor as I began to sob.

All I'd ever wanted was for Oliver Stanhope to want me. To love me. To be his.

But after all we'd been through, how could that ever be my dream again?

I sat outside on the bench, waiting for the bus. I didn't want to spend extra money on a ride-share app, and Gillian was at her job with her car. My mother had begged me to go to lunch with her and had offered to pick me up, but I wanted to be able to leave if I needed to.

I wasn't thrilled at the idea of having lunch with her but I knew I should give her a chance.

I was nervous as hell. My mom had never been very close to me. She had done everything with my sister. Seeing her again made me feel like the same sad, rejected kid.

When I arrived at Joe's Diner, she was already sitting down. She stood up and waved at me when I walked in and I smiled weakly, sliding into the seat across from her.

"You look great, Lexie," she said. My mother was the person who had given me the nickname and it made my heart clench to hear her say it.

"Thank you," I mumbled. We ordered our drinks and entrees at the same time because we'd been coming to Joe's for years and knew the menu front and back.

"I'm so glad you were willing to meet up," she said, smiling. "It's been so long since you've been close enough to visit."

I nodded slowly. "It's good to see you, Mom."

"You said on the phone there was something you wanted to tell me?"

I licked my lips nervously. "There is." I put a hand on my stomach. "I think I'm going to move away from Wagontown pretty soon." I put my hand on my belly.

She froze. "What?"

Her face was expressionless.

"I'm due in August," I told her. "I want to have my new life sorted out by then."

"What about Ollie?" she asked flatly.

I drew in a deep breath through my nose. "He still doesn't trust me. I just can't do this with him breathing down my neck. He can come visit our child once in a while if he wants."

"Oliver?" she gasped. "That doesn't seem like him. He was always crazy about you and he has a son now, so he understands what parenting is all about."

"We're not together," I said quickly. "He doesn't love me."

"But you're pregnant. Lexie, how could you do that to him?"

I stared at her. "How could I what?"

"Why would you keep your child from its father? That's just cruel." I sighed. This felt like so many other of our conversations. I felt the old bitterness creeping up. "Mom, you just don't actually care about me, do you? You're always thinking of someone else. It's always that I'm inconveniencing everyone else."

" This is going to ruin your life, Lexie."

I stood up, not caring that the food hadn't arrived. "Great, Mom. Really great. Thanks."

"Lexie, sit back down. I—"

"You don't get to tell me what to do. Not here, and not about this baby," I snapped. "You've never been there for me. Never. When Oliver and I broke up and I cried myself to sleep every night, all you could talk about was how I wasn't doing as well as Gillian."

"Lexie..."

"Stop it, Mom. You don't even know me. You shouldn't even call me by my nickname. I reserve that right for friends."

"Oh, really? I'm the one who named you, aren't I?"

"That's about all you did." I sneered and stalked out of the diner, walking quickly to the bus stop.

Mom didn't bother to follow me. Typical.

I closed my eyes tightly against the tears but they started to fall anyway. I called the only person I could think of that might help me. I couldn't get on the bus while sobbing.

"Hello?" Tristan answered, and I choked back a sob.

"Can you come pick me up from the bus stop near Joe's?" I managed, my voice shaking and thick.

"Lex, of course. What's wrong?"

"Just please come get me," I pleaded.

"Of course. Be there in a minute."

Tristan hung up the phone and I broke down, putting my head in my hands and sobbing into them.

He arrived within ten minutes. He ushered me to the car, opening the door for me.

"What happened?" he asked when he got into the driver's seat.

"I had lunch with my mother," I deadpanned, and Tristan snorted.

"That'll do it."

He knew how much my mother and I had fought when I was a teenager. At least my dad mostly ignored me. My mother was always criticizing me. God, when I thought about it, Dick was the same way.

Everything I did was always under scrutiny.

"How are your parents?" I asked, trying to change the subject. But I already knew that Tristan and his parents didn't get along, either.

He shrugged. "I guess they're doing okay. I don't speak to them anymore."

I took in a shaking breath. "I'm beginning to think I never should have started talking to Mom again."

He nodded. "I can understand that."

"Could you take me to the Pig? I need to pick up my check."

"Of course," he said easily, smiling at me. "You know, Oliver called me."

My eyes widened. "He did?"

"Yeah. We had a beer together. He apologized to me," he admitted.

"That's... that's crazy," I murmured. I didn't think Oliver had it in him to admit he was wrong, to Tristan, of all people.

"I forgave him," he said quietly. "And I think you should, too."

"Tristan," I started just as we arrived at the Pig. I put the rest of it on hold because he wanted to come in with me to order food. I realized I was starving since I had left Joe's before my food came.

I knew I looked terrible, my eyes puffy, but Raoul didn't say a word. He just smiled at me as Tristan and I sat down at the bar.

"What'll it be?"

"A ginger ale and ten wings. With sweet potato fries, please," I ordered quickly.

"Sure thing, sweetheart. I'll put it under your employee discount." He looked to Tristan. "And for your boyfriend?"

Tristan laughed. "Not a boyfriend. Just a best friend." He put an arm around my shoulders and squeezed before ordering himself a burger and regular fries along with a soda.

He still had his arm around me when Oliver came out of the office. He froze when he saw us, and my heart started to pound.

I had no idea what he would do. I had to admit, it scared me to death the way he went after Tristan last time. Dick was a violent man beneath the surface, and he'd been scary at times, too.

I didn't want that for me and Oliver, I didn't want to be afraid of him.

To my relief, Oliver just smiled and walked toward us, sitting next to Tristan.

"The Three Musketeers, back together again," he said happily, glancing at me for a brief second.

I sighed in relief. He was acting civil about this, even like we were all friends again.

I felt Tristan tense up when Oliver first approached but he quickly relaxed when Oliver sat next to him.

"I can't believe you bought the Pig," he groaned. "You took out all the dank and dive out of this place."

"Isn't it so much better, though?" Oliver replied.

"I miss the dank," Tristan teased, and Oliver laughed out loud.

God, it was good to see them like that. It made my heart soar. I hadn't seen Oliver and Tristan together as friends in so long.

"When am I going to be Uncle Tristan?" he asked, smiling at me, and I put a hand on my stomach.

"August."

"I can't wait. A summer baby."

I groaned. "I'm going to be so big and miserable in the heat."

"I'll make sure the air conditioner is working great by then," Oliver said. He cleared his throat. "Speaking of that... there's an issue with the breakers at the cabin. I'd like to take a look, if that's okay. I figured you'll be coming back from your sister's place soon, to start preparing the nursery and stuff."

Tristan stared at Oliver, grinning. There was some telepathic connection going on between them and I narrowed my eyes.

"What are you two up to?"

"No good," they said in unison, like they always did before, and we all laughed.

We ate and chatted for a while, teasing Tristan about his love for old vinyl albums and even older cars, then started throwing out baby names.

"What about Adam?" Oliver asked. "After my grandfather."

"That's perfect," I breathed, smiling at him. He smiled back, causing that dimple in his cheek to pop out.

"If it's a boy, that is," I said. I looked away, flushing. I couldn't help that I was still so attracted to him.

I cleared my throat. "I should head home," I said.

Oliver sighed. "Yeah, me too. I need to pick up Trent."

"How's his fever?"

"Much better, thanks," Oliver said, giving me a little half-smile.

Tristan looked between me and Oliver. "Am I interrupting something?"

"Absolutely not," I said at the same time Oliver replied, "maybe."

I groaned and stood up. "You're not interrupting a thing, Tristan," I said, glaring a little at Oliver, his face falling. I felt a little bad and softened. "Let me know when you want to look at the breakers. Can I get my check?"

"Oh. Yeah, of course," Oliver muttered. He headed to the office then returned with my paycheck. After another round of goodbyes, Tristan and I left the bar, heading back to the cabin.

We sat on the porch for a while, catching up, and it felt like old times all over again. I was getting back some of the things I lost all those years ago, and it felt good.

The only thing missing was Oliver.

But could I forgive him?

Chapter 28

Oliver

I spent an hour figuring out what to wear on the day I was scheduled to go over to the cabin to "check the breakers." I didn't want to wear anything too fancy, because then she'd know I was up to something. She already seemed to suspect something when we discussed it at the Pig.

I had to talk to her, had to be around her. There was something about Lex that was so overwhelmingly... Lex. And I craved it. I wanted it, needed it, as much as I needed food and water.

I finally decided on a pair of jeans and a simple V-neck shirt. I ran a hand through my hair to tame it.

I knocked on the door of the cabin after taking in a long breath. After a few minutes, Lex answered.

She blinked at me with tired eyes. "Why are you here so early?" she groaned.

I looked at my watch. It was seven in the morning.

I winced. "Sorry, I just wanted to get this taken care of," I lied.

She moved aside and let me in. The whole cabin

217

smelled like her. I wanted to breathe it in, breathe her in, but I had "work" to do.

I went down to the cellar to check the breakers, flipping them on and off, turning off appliances and lights all over the cabin.

I had no idea what I was doing.

Lex came down after a few minutes. "This seems a bit excessive," she complained.

"It's important," I insisted. "If there's a short somewhere, it could set the cabin on fire."

Lexie sighed, crossing her arms over her chest, and leaning against the cellar door.

"Are you really here to check the breakers or because you want to talk to me?" she asked flatly.

I froze, turning to look at her, the answer written all over my face.

She was showing now. She looked amazing. Her skin was glowing. Her green eyes were brighter than ever. Her breasts were swollen and there was a little baby bump all because she was pregnant with my baby....

God, I wanted her. Wanted to take her right there in the cellar. But unfortunately, she headed back up into the cabin and I followed her without even thinking.

I'd follow her to hell if she asked me to.

I sat down in the recliner in the living room, and she stood in front of me, glaring.

"If you're done with the breakers, you can go," she muttered.

"I'm not going anywhere," I said firmly. "This is my place."

"Don't throw that in my face, Oliver," she snapped. "You allowed me to live here. You wanted me to live here, didn't you?"

I huffed out a breath. "I want you close, can't you see that?"

"Why? We're just friends, right?" Her tone was sharp, but I could hear the hurt in it.

I groan. "That was stupid of me to say, Lexie. How many times do I need to apologize? We could never be just friends and you know it. Because we're in love."

She stared at me, her eyes wide. "We are? This is the first I'm hearing of it."

I leaned forward, putting my forearms on my thighs. "You can't tell me that you don't feel what I feel, Lex. I can't stand being away from you. I can't stand seeing you around town, pregnant with my baby, and knowing you aren't mine. It's killing me."

"What are you saying, Oliver?" she asked in a shaky voice. I noticed she was trembling, and I reached out to grab her wrist, pulling her into my lap. She instantly straddled me. We'd sat like this so many times before, with her wrapped around me, while I was emailing someone or on the phone. She'd always wanted to be close to me.

I pressed my forehead to hers. "I love you, Lex. I love you so much and I always have."

"Love was never the problem with us," she whispered. "Trust was."

"I want you to trust me again. Trust me like I trust you."

"Oliver," she groaned, and she opened her mouth to argue but I grabbed her by the back of the head, pulling her down to press my lips against hers. Despite her anger, she parted her lips instantly, and I delved my tongue into her mouth.

She made a little whimpering sound as she rocked her hips against my growing erection and I groaned, kissing her throat, nibbling little bites up and down her neck.

"I can't trust you," she said breathlessly. "I can't trust that you won't leave me again. I can't trust that you won't get jealous and try to control me."

With that she pulled away and stood up, leaving me sitting there, panting, as she left the room. I stayed that way for a long moment, thinking.

A memory washed over me.

Lex came in with tears streaking down her cheeks, her face puffy and her eyes haunted. She slid under the garage door, like she always did, so my dad wouldn't know she was here.

"Lex," I said. "What happened?"

She threw herself into my arms, hugging me tightly and sobbing into my neck.

"It's Mom. We had a huge fight. She kicked me out for the night. Said I could find somewhere else to sleep."

I huffed out a breath. "I need to have a conversation with your mother."

She shook her head. "It won't help," she mumbled. "She doesn't love me. She only loves Gillian."

"I'm sure that's not true, honey—" I started, but she cut me off, pulling away from me and pacing around the garage.

"You don't get it, Ollie," she said, sniffling. "You don't understand. Your dad might be hard on you, but at least you know your parents love you. Mine kicked me out over a disagreement. My dad is never home and even when he is, he acts like I don't exist. And my mother..." Her voice trembled and she took in a breath before speaking again. "My mother hates me."

She looked at me with incredibly sad green eyes, and my breath caught in my throat. I loved her more in that moment than I ever had. I wanted to protect her from everything, including her family.

220

"You're all I have," she said softly, coming close to me. "You won't ever leave me, will you, Ollie?"

"Of course not," I said fiercely, and I couldn't imagine ever breaking that promise.

But I did. And I did it all without talking to her first, without asking her if the allegations were true. I rubbed a hand across my face and stood up, walking into the kitchen where Lex was crying softly, her face in her hands.

"I'm so sorry I hurt you, Lex," I said quietly. She didn't turn around, didn't look at me. My heart ached. "I just hope that someday you can forgive me. Because I don't know if I can live without you."

I quietly walked out of the cabin. She didn't follow me.

Walking back up to my house felt like walking to the gallows.

* * *

An agonizing week later, I got a text from Lexie.

Ultrasound appointment this afternoon. 2 p.m.

The next text was an address downtown.

I drew in a deep breath. I could do this. I could co-parent with Lexie and accept that there would be nothing else between us.

When I dropped Trent off at my mother's house, she stopped me at the door. "You bring back some pictures of that baby," she demanded, and I couldn't help but laugh.

"I will, Mom."

She hugged me goodbye, and I walked to the car hurriedly, because I was running a little late.

Lexie was already there, frowning and watching the door as I walked in. Her face relaxed when she saw me. I took that as a plus, anyway.

I cleared my throat and sat next to her, shifting in my seat. "How have you been feeling?"

"Fine, just tired," she answered flatly, and my heart ached for her. She was pregnant, she shouldn't be working two jobs when I could comfortably pay for things But it's what she wanted to do. She was saving up to leave.

The idea of her leaving made panic claw at my throat but I pushed it down. I had to focus on the baby.

I missed every ultrasound for Trent. I missed the entire pregnancy. I wanted to be here for every second of this one.

The nurse called Lexie back and I followed, waiting patiently while she changed into the gown.

"I'm nervous," she admitted, shifting on the hospital bed.

"It's going to be okay," I promised her. "Our baby is strong and healthy; I just know it."

She smiled, taking my hand, and it made my heart soar.

The ultrasound tech smiled at us as she moved the wand around Lexie's belly. I was shocked by how strong the heartbeat was, how loud it sounded in the room.

"Here we are," the tech said. "Your baby's head, and arms..."

She pointed everything out and the baby was beautiful. It was just a tiny profile but what a profile it was. They had Lexie's nose.

"Do you want to know the sex?"

Lexie looked at me, tears in her green eyes. "Do we?"

"I do," I said and squeezed her hand. "But if you don't, we can wait."

"I want to know," Lexie said excitedly, looking at the tech.

"It's a girl," the ultrasound tech said, smiling. My heart swelled in my chest.

A little girl. A little girl with Lexie's nose and maybe her pretty green eyes.

Tears streamed down my face, and Lexie wiped them away as the doctor came in.

"Everything looks perfect. You're measuring well for six months, and the baby is a good size. Strong heartbeat. Healthy."

"Can I ask a question, doctor?" I asked. Lexie frowned at me slightly, but I had to know.

"Of course."

"Is it dangerous for her to work so much? Heading into the third trimester?"

"She should be fine to work right up until the eighth month, but then she'll have to take it easy," he warned. "And even now, she shouldn't be overworking, or on her feet too much. She needs her rest."

Lexie glared at me, but I was worried about what the doctor had said.

"You're quitting your jobs," I said flatly when we got outside, laden with ultrasound pictures.

"Hell, no, I'm not," Lexie shot back.

"You heard what the doctor said!"

"Did *you* hear what he said? Because he said I could work right up until my eighth month," she said smugly.

I frowned at her, feeling frustrated. Lexie could push my buttons unlike anyone else.

"Then at least quit one of them. The grocery job. I'll help my grandmother fill your position."

Lexie sighed heavily. "All right, fine. But I'm working out my two weeks' notice."

I nodded. "Deal. And by the way, I'm driving you home," I added, knowing she had taken the bus there.

Back at the cabin, Lexie got out of the car with a grunt. I called her name.

She turned to look at me. "What?"

"I love you," I said, and she blinked, looking shocked, before she headed inside.

I couldn't help but grin at the flush on her cheeks.

She still wanted me.

She had to.

Because I needed her.

Chapter 29

Lexie

Oliver's words kept echoing in my mind.

I love you.

He'd said it. Not spoken around it, not hinted at it. He'd actually said the words.

But did he mean them? That was the real question.

Before the pregnancy, Oliver would show up to the Pig maybe three times a week. Now he was coming in every shift I worked. Granted, he stayed in the office most of the time and didn't bother me much, but still. I knew that he was watching out for me. I found it a little irritating, but I also found it a bit sweet.

I worked out my two weeks at the grocery store, leaving Oliver's grandmother with a teary-eyed hug. She'd taken a chance on me, and I hoped I'd proven myself useful for her, if even for a short time.

I'd been having a weird feeling lately whenever Gillian and I were headed to the Pig, like someone was following us. After Dick had showed up there, I guess I was worried that he'd do it again someday. Seeing how things had ended,

I wouldn't be surprised if Dick showed up in places when I least expected it.

Gillian dropped me off, frowning at the look on my face.

"You look pale," she said. "Are you sure you're okay? Did you eat this morning?"

I winced. "I didn't have time."

Gillian opened her mouth, likely to scold me, but I held up a hand.

"I promise I'll eat at work," I told her. And I meant it. I wanted to do right by this baby, and taking care of myself was part of that.

She nodded, but she was still frowning when I shut the door and walked inside.

Krista met me inside. "Thank God you're here. The bar is full already. Tourists," she said that last part as if there were rats sitting at the bar instead of patrons.

I chuckled. "Let me grab a bite and then I'll get started."

"Of course." She looked down at my swollen belly. "Gotta keep that baby fed."

Krista smiled at me brightly and I smiled back. She'd become a friend in the months that I'd worked at the Pig.

I headed back to the kitchen and peeked around the corner at the cook, Larry.

"Larry," I called in a sing-song voice. "Could I have some bacon loaded fries?"

He looked up, slight irritation on his face until he saw who it was. He broke into an instant smile.

"Anything for you, sweetheart."

Larry and I got along great. I was always helpful in the kitchen whenever they got slammed, and I always treated him with high regard and respect.

He wasted no time cooking my food, and I hurriedly

ate, not allowing the fries to cool down first. I breathed in and out quickly trying not to burn my tongue, my cheeks puffing out.

When I was about halfway finished, Raoul came back, a worried look on his face.

"Raoul, what's wrong?" I asked, rubbing my hands on my apron.

"I'm so behind," he gasped, and my shoulders slumped in relief. A part of me had been worried that Dick had shown up again. "I have like ten drinks to make and more orders are coming in—"

I cut him off with a hand on his shoulder. "It's okay, Raoul. I'm ready. Tell me what drinks you need."

He rattled them off and I scribbled them down on my server book. "Got it. I'll make all the drinks, don't worry. You grab the orders then tell me where they go. Okay?"

He sighed. "Thank God for you, Lex." He hurried off to get the orders and I all but jogged toward the bar. Krista was behind it, pouring drinks expertly.

"I'm helping Raoul get caught up, but I'll help you next, promise," I told her. Krista nodded curtly in response. She was in the zone.

I managed to pour all of Raoul's drinks before he got back and he hugged me quickly from behind.

"You're the best, Lex. I hope you never leave."

I swallowed hard, not wanting to tell him that I was planning to get out of here as soon as possible.

I just smiled at him. "Thanks. I try."

He rushed off to deliver the drinks. Raoul and Krista had both been angels about my pregnancy, doing most of the running around and making sure I took frequent breaks to get off my feet.

Krista and I focused on the patrons sitting at the bar as

Raoul worked the tables, and by the time we were finished, it was nearly two in the morning. Time had flown by, and I was absolutely exhausted, but our tips were great and that gave me a big boost.

I was cleaning the outside of the bar when the door dinged. We weren't quite closed yet, and if someone just wanted a quick drink, I'd be happy to serve them. Raoul and Krista had already left, and I was the last one in the building.

At least, I thought I was. We had been so busy all night I had no idea if Oliver was back in the office.

I turned around and my mouth dropped open in shock. Dick stood there, swaying on his feet.

"Come back to me," he slurred, and this time, there wasn't anger in his voice, only hurt.

I braced myself against the bar, my heart pounding, fear settling in. "Dick," I said softly. "You're drunk. Let me call you a cab."

I was scared, knowing his mood could change in a second, especially when he was inebriated. But I hoped I'd be able to talk him into leaving before I'd need to call the cops. I wished with all my might that Raoul and Krista were still there.

"Our anniversary is tomorrow," he said, getting closer to me. "Come home with me," he pleaded, his eyes wet.

"Dick. You can't keep doing this."

He glanced down at my stomach, his eyes showing recognition "You're pregnant. Is it mine?"

"No, Dick," I replied quickly, and he frowned, getting even closer. I kept my hands on the bar, hoping that I could sprint sideways if he got too close.

"So who have you been sleeping with then?" he demanded, but again, he didn't seem angry.

"Dick—"

"I don't care," he cut me off. "I'll raise the baby as my own. We're perfect together, Lex. We work well together. I want you back in my life. I want you back so badly."

"You don't love me," I said flatly. "And I don't love you."

He scoffed. "What is love, anyway? Didn't you once tell me that love was just a fairy tale? Just something that people prayed for, but they never got?"

I bit my lip. He was right. I used to think that, after Oliver broke up with me. I thought that settling for Dick was the only way I could have stability. But now that Oliver was back in my life things were different. Even though I was angry at him, I no longer believed that love was just a fairy tale. I knew it was real, even if it hurt.

"I don't believe that anymore," I told him, being completely honest. Dick might have been bad for me, hell, we were bad for each other, but there were moments when he was sweet to me. He deserved to know the truth. "I'm in love with someone else."

"That bastard who threw me out?" Dick shot back as he grabbed my arm, dragging me toward the door. In that moment, all the breath seemed to go out of my body.

"Help!" I screamed, hoping that Larry might still be in the kitchen, that somebody, anybody, would hear me.

This Dick was a different man, a dangerous one. He was showing another side of himself, one I had suspected lurked beneath the surface all along.

My instinct to protect my baby kicked in, and I wrenched away from him, running toward the back exit.

I was going to make it. I could see the door of the exit; it was so close.

Dick grabbed me around the waist, and I screamed again.

My head spun. What was I going to do?

Chapter 30

Oliver

I was deep in paperwork when I heard Lexie scream.

I had been hiding in the office all night. I didn't want to see Lexie. Well, I did want to see her, but I knew she didn't want to see me. I didn't know how she would react or if she'd even talk to me. I didn't know how she would react or if she'd even talk to me. I didn't know how she would react or if she'd even talk to me. Things hadn't ended well between us the last time we spoke.

But as soon as I heard her scream, I jerked open the office door, running into the bar area as quickly as I could.

Dick had her around the waist, dragging her toward the door.

"Oliver!" she shouted.

I rushed Dick, grabbing his shoulder and shoving him off of Lexie. Lexie ran toward the bar, grabbing her phone and calling 911.

"You bastard," Dick said, throwing a punch, but he was too drunk, and it was easy to take him down. I pushed him to the ground, pulling his arm behind him. "You're going to break my arm!" he yelled.

"Then I guess you shouldn't treat women the way you do."

"You got my fiancée pregnant," he scowled. "I should kill you."

"You can try," I replied as I sat on his back, not quite breaking his arm but causing tremendous pain. He yelped and tried to wriggle free but I was bigger than him. He was also inebriated so his reflexes weren't as quick.

The cops arrived in less than five minutes, the sheriff's office was just down the street.

Reese walked in ready with a pair of handcuffs dangling from his hand, the blue and red lights flashing brightly, hurting my eyes.

"I've got it from here, Ollie," Reese said flatly, and I stood up. Dick scrambled toward the back exit as soon as I got off him, but Reese ran him down, grabbing him and slamming him against the wall.

"You're being arrested for trespassing," Reese said. "You have the right to remain silent—"

"And assault," I piped up, hurrying over to Lexie, who was sitting on a bar stool, trembling.

I put a hand on her arm, and she winced. A bruise was already forming where Dick had grabbed her.

"The baby—"

"I'm okay," she said quickly. "He didn't touch anywhere else, just my arm."

"We should go to the hospital just in case," I told her, and she nodded slowly.

"The doctor did tell me to avoid stress," she said with a dark chuckle.

"Our little girl will be fine," I said quickly, wanting to reassure her while my heart pounded out of my chest.

An ambulance arrived just a few moments after Reese. The dispatcher must have called both, and I was grateful.

I rode in the back of the ambulance with Lexie, taking her hand in mine.

"What if something is wrong?" she asked worriedly. "What if the stress—"

"Everything is going to be just fine," I said firmly. "Don't even talk like that. The baby's going to be fine. *You're* going to be fine."

One good thing about living in a small town was that there wasn't much hospital traffic, and Lexie was in a hospital bed hooked up to monitors in no time.

She watched the fetal monitor with worry, biting her bottom lip. I reached over and gently rubbed her face.

"Strong heartbeat," I pointed out. "Just like before."

She nodded slowly, smiling slightly. "Thanks to you," she said softly.

"I'm just glad I was in the office." I frowned. "You're not allowed to be the last person in the bar ever again. In fact, I want you to quit."

She blinked at me. "Quit?"

"I want to take care of you," I said quietly. "You and the baby. I know that you don't want me—"

"Oliver..."

I cut her off. "Look, you can stay living in the cabin, and I won't bother you. Just let me pay for everything, at least until after the baby's born. I know that you're proud, Lex, but *please*, let me do this."

She opened her mouth to speak but a doctor walked in, halting her words.

I turned, looking toward him, a hopeful expression on my face.

"Miss Tripp, everything seems to be in order here," he said in a no-nonsense tone. "You've got some bruises, but they'll heal, and nothing is fractured. The baby seems fine."

"Thank God," Lexie breathed. "I appreciate it, doctor."

He smiled. "Just take it easy. It might be a good idea to get off your feet for a few days."

Lexie nodded, and the doctor left.

"I'm serious, Lex," I told her. "I don't want you to work anymore."

"Okay," she said quietly, just as I was teeing up to argue some more.

"Wait, what? Okay?"

"Okay, Ollie," she said, smiling a little. "I'll quit. But you'll have a hard time finding someone as good as me to take my place," she said proudly, squeezing my hand.

"You're one of a kind, that's for sure," I murmured, bringing her hand to my lips, and kissing along her knuckles.

She kept smiling at me and I considered that a win. As much as I hated that asshole showing up and scaring her, I was relieved she was all right and glad she was talking to me. Glad she was letting me touch her.

The nurse came in with the discharge papers and I helped Lex get up and dressed. I wanted to carry her out to the car, but something told me she wouldn't allow that, so I just held her hand tightly, pulling her close to me.

"Take me home," Lexie said as we got into the car, and I nodded in agreement. When I pulled up to the cabin, however, Lexie didn't immediately get out when I opened her door.

"Lex?"

"Come inside," she said quietly. I helped her get out of the car and followed her wordlessly, having no idea what was going on.

She unlocked the door, and we went inside. I closed and locked it behind us.

Lexie turned to look at me then, her green eyes wide and wet with unshed tears.

"I'm sorry, Oliver," she whispered, the tears spilling out and down her cheeks.

"Oh, honey." I put my hands on her shoulders. "None of this was your fault. Not a single moment of it."

"Not just about tonight," she insisted, sniffling. "But... everything. I shouldn't have dismissed you when you told me how you felt. When you apologized."

"What are you saying?" I stuttered, hope starting to take flight in my stomach and chest. My heart clenched.

"I'm saying that I love you too, Ollie. I always have. I always will."

I searched her face, looking for any kind of hesitancy, and found none. She looked up at me with wide eyes.

"I forgive you for what happened back then. Can you forgive me for how I've acted lately?" she asked shakily.

"You're serious, Lex? You—"

"I love you," she said fiercely. "I've always been in love with you since the moment we met. I never stopped. I thought about you every single day while we were apart—"

I cut her off by grabbing the back of her head and pulling her close to kiss her passionately.

The kiss was rough and sudden, and when I touched her, my fingers barely touched her skin, only wanting to love her, to cherish her.

Lexie pulled away from me after a moment but when I started to protest, she took my hand with a small smile, leading me to the bedroom.

She began to undress slowly, and I couldn't help but admire her as the goddess that she was. I worshipped the ground she walked on. I loved her so much I didn't know what to do with it, didn't know how to say it.

"Lexie," I mumbled as she finally stood bare before me, her belly swollen, her breasts bigger than before. "You're so beautiful."

She flushed slightly, pouting, and pulling at my shirt. I took it off with one hand, already growing hard from the way she was looking at me.

Her hands went to my waistband, unbuttoning my slacks and unzipping them. She shoved her hand down my pants and groped me over my boxer briefs, and I moaned so loudly that if we had any close neighbor's, they surely would have heard loud and clear.

"Oliver," she crooned. "Make love to me."

Make love to me. Not *I want you inside of me* or anything crude, just... love.

I would show her how much I cared. How I worshipped her.

I let my slacks fall to the floor, stepping out of them along with my shoes, and Lexie sat down on the bed, watching me hungrily.

She hooked her thumbs into either side of my waistband and pulled down my boxer briefs, freeing me. I hissed as the cool air hit my heated erection, but soon enough she was taking me into her mouth. I froze, putting a hand in her hair gently.

She moaned, and I let her place her lips around me for just a few moments before I gently pulled away.

"You're going to make me come if you keep that up," I gasped. Lexie smiled wickedly.

She laid back on the bed, scooting up toward the head-board and spreading her thighs. I looked down at her, how she was glistening, and my mouth was nearly watering.

I slid between her legs but she leaned forward, grabbing at my shoulders.

"Not tonight," she said. "I just want you close, Ollie."

My heart warmed in my chest, and I covered her with my body, my erection pressing up against her hip.

"I've wanted this for so long," I murmured. "I don't know if I'll last long."

"Me either." And then she giggled, and it made me feel drunk, like her laughter was a drug that made my head spin.

I chuckled and moved to guide myself inside her. She locked her legs around my waist, her belly pressing up against my pelvis. I froze.

"This won't hurt the baby, will it?" I asked with a frown.

Lexie groaned. "Of course not. I've done my research. Sex is okay and often encouraged."

I laughed out loud. "I'm glad you've done your homework."

I slid into her, and she was so slick and hot it made the back of my neck tingle. I paused for a moment, looking down into her eyes, which were still brimming with tears, before I started to move.

Tears pricked at my own eyes when she let out a sob of my name.

"I love you so much," she managed, her voice shaky. I leaned down to kiss her softly as I started to roll my hips faster, chasing my orgasm, chasing how wonderful she made me feel.

It was like every part of me was on fire, and I couldn't help myself from kissing her again before moving my mouth to her throat, murmuring against her skin.

"You're the only woman I've ever loved, Lex. You're the only woman I'll ever love."

She sobbed out another moan. "I'm so close, Ollie, please, don't stop."

I didn't, moving faster and faster until my head felt like

it might explode from the pleasure. Lexie began to clench around me, gasping in air, and soon enough, I was spilling inside her.

I moaned against her neck, not wanting it to be over, but Lexie was mewling out little moans and still clenching around me. It felt so good I kept moving inside her.

I started to harden again after just a few moments, and Lexie giggled. "Again?" She chided me.

I actually blushed. "We don't have to..." I stuttered, but she pulled me closer, lifting her hips up to pull me deeper inside of her.

"Shut up and love me," she whispered.

I moved slowly this time, kissing her neck, her shoulders, drawing back to give her swollen, sensitive breasts attention.

She arched off the bed when I drew her breasts into my mouth, one at a time, her fingers curling in my hair. "I didn't know pregnancy sex would be like this," she admitted, her breathing a bit rough.

"Like what?" I managed to reply, drawing closer to my release.

"So incredible," she told me, just before she orgasmed, her pussy clenching around me and causing me to tumble after her. I was shaking so hard I thought I might fall on her, but I managed to balance above her, enjoying the sight of her pleasure as my own orgasm flooded through me.

Overstimulated, I pulled out of her, lying next to her on the bed. She moved to curl into me immediately, putting her head on my chest.

"You're everything to me, you know that? You, Trent, and our little girl," I said fiercely, and she nodded against my chest.

"I know that now," she said. "I just wish I'd realized it a long time ago."

We laid there in silence for another long moment before I looked over and noticed she was biting her lip.

"What's wrong?"

"What if Trent hates me?" she asked. "What if he thinks I'm trying to replace his mother—"

I cut her off. "Do you know what he asked me when I told him he'd have another brother or sister?"

She shook her head, still biting her lip.

"He asked me if that meant he'd have a mommy, too," I said, and Lexie's eyes filled with tears again.

"He did?"

I nodded. "And you'll be a wonderful mother, Lex. To both our children."

"You really think so?"

"I know so." I hugged her close to me.

I didn't know she had fallen asleep until she started snoring, and I couldn't help but chuckle in the back of my throat. She'd always snored like a trucker.

I fell asleep with the ease of a man who knew his life was perfect.

Chapter 31

Lexie

I woke up in Oliver's arms, and for once, I didn't want to bolt. I kissed his cheek, and when he didn't wake, I kissed his jawline, his nose, his mouth.

He woke up with a snort, startled, and I giggled.

"Oh no," he muttered. "Trent."

My eyes widened. "He spent the night at his grandmother's, remember?"

Oliver nodded. "That's right. I've got to get over there." He paused. "Will you go with me?"

I bit my lip. "I don't know. We don't want to spring this on him out of nowhere, do we?"

"No time like the present."

I was nervous as hell. I'd barely met Trent, what if he didn't like me? What if he was jealous of my time with his father or jealous of his little sister?

Oliver thumbed my bottom lip out from between my teeth and I pouted. He laughed and kissed my mouth before swinging his legs over the side of the bed.

"It's going to be fine. Trent takes things in stride. He's a pretty chill kid."

"I know but—"

Oliver turned to kiss me again, shutting me up. "No buts."

"Okay," I sighed, and got up with a grunt. I went to my closet, groaning when I realized I barely had any clothes that fit anymore. "I'm too fat to wear anything," I moaned.

"What? You're not fat, Lex, you're pregnant. And glowing."

I narrowed my eyes at him. "Don't get too close, I could be radioactive."

He barked out a laugh and got up, coming over to put his arms around my waist from behind, locking them just below my breasts, which were swollen and aching from the pregnancy.

"I'll buy you some maternity clothes," he said. "For now, why don't you wear that little milkmaid dress of yours? The one with the polka dots."

"You remember that dress?"

"You wore it to pick up your check from work last week. You looked incredible in it," he murmured, kissing my neck, biting gently at my collarbone.

"Don't do that," I groaned. "We'll be even later than we already are."

We were up so late last night that we had slept past noon.

Oliver let me go with a chuckle and dressed in his clothes from the night before, picking his phone up from the nightstand.

"We have to go," he said quickly. "My mom has some-where to be.".

I hurried to get dressed and grabbed my purse, following him and frowning.

"Are you sure I should go?"

241

"You go where I go, Alexandra Tripp," Oliver said, smiling weakly at me, and I wondered what was wrong.

We arrived at his mother's place in record time, with Oliver driving a bit over the speed limit.

Oliver helped me out of the car and we walked hand in hand up to the door. He knocked quickly, letting go of my hand.

I looked over at him, confused, but then his mother opened the door.

"Oh, thank goodness you're here," she said with a sigh. "Trent's been so worried."

Trent came running down the stairs, slamming into his father and grabbing him around the waist.

"I thought you left," he sobbed as Oliver picked him up.

"I would never leave you, buddy," Oliver said quietly, and I just stood there, feeling awkward, unsure what was happening.

"He gets like this sometimes," Oliver's mother explained, ushering me into the kitchen. "I've made some tea."

I paused at the door when I saw Oliver's father sitting at the kitchen table with a cup of tea.

"Oh. Hello."

Oliver came into the kitchen with Trent, who still had his head buried in his father's chest.

"What are you doing here?" Oliver growled.

His father held his hands up in defence. "I'm just here to see your mother. She needed some help calming Trent down."

"And you weren't available," Oliver's mother added, but there was no bite to her tone as she smiled at me. "Do you like sugar or cream?"

"Just sugar, please," I responded quietly, looking at Oliver's father. He'd asked me for forgiveness, but I wasn't sure if I was going to give it to him. Forgiving Oliver was different than forgiving his father. His father was the ultimate reason for our breakup, and for Oliver and Tristan's falling out.

I slowly sat down at the table and Oliver did the same, still holding Trent.

Oliver opened his mouth to speak but I patted his knee, looking at him. "It's okay, Ollie," I told him, and he relaxed.

"Oliver, this is as good a time as any to tell you," his mother began, pouring my tea and adding three sugar cubes, "that your father is moving back in."

Oliver froze. "What?"

"He and I have had a few long conversations." She looked at me. "One or two of them about you, Lexie."

"Me?" I asked, confused.

"One of the reasons we separated was because I found out about what he did back then."

She glared at her husband, and he hung his head.

"But we've gotten past it," he said softly.

"We're *trying* to get past it," she corrected, sitting next to me. "But you and this grandchild are a big reason why we're reconnecting."

"Good," I said, smiling. "Because I'm sure Trent and the new baby will love knowing their grandparents are together."

Trent lifted his head; tear tracks staining his face. "Are you going to be my new mommy?" he asked quietly, and my heart ached.

"If that's what you want," I said slowly, not wanting to push.

Trent was quiet for a moment and then his face broke into a big smile before he fell over into my arms.

I caught him, surprised, and hugged him tightly while laughing.

"I think that's a yes," Oliver said with a chuckle, and I felt tears pricking at the backs of my eyes as I looked at him.

Oliver smiled.

We sat and chatted with his parents for the better part of an hour, and although things were still tense between Oliver and his dad, they seemed better by the time we left.

I was grateful. All I'd ever wanted was for Oliver's family to like me, and it seemed like we were on the right track.

I felt amazing as we drove off in the car, looking out the window, unable to stop smiling.

"Daddy, can we go get ice cream?" Trent asked.

"Kiddo, it's lunch time."

Trent pouted.

"We could go get lunch first," I suggested. "And then ice cream after?" I looked at Oliver, mirroring Trent's pout.

"Two against one," Oliver groaned.

I rubbed my belly. "Two soon to be three," I said with a wink.

Trent bounced around in his car seat. "Can we? Can we?"

"All right, all right," Oliver conceded. "The diner?"

"Let's go someplace different," I suggested. "What about that new family place on Third? The one with the arcade?"

Trent gasped. "An *arcade*?"

Oliver smiled at him in the rearview mirror. "Let's do it."

Trent whooped in victory.

We arrived at the restaurant and were seated right away. Trent kept staring at the arcade area.

"We have to eat our food first, okay, buddy?" I said, and Trent sighed heavily. But then he looked at me with a smile.

"Okay, Mommy."

Tears sprang to my eyes, and I sniffled, wiping at them as my heart just seemed to swell and swell.

"Are you all right?" Oliver asked quietly.

"I'm perfect," I said. "Everything is... perfect."

"It is, isn't it?" he agreed.

Trent leaned his head against my shoulder for a moment, smiling, before coloring his kid's menu.

An hour later, Trent and I were playing Pac-Man on the arcade machine, and he was beating my pants off.

"You're too good at this," I complained.

He laughed out loud. "I'm just good enough, Daddy always says."

"Daddy can kick both your butts at Pac-Man," Oliver said, coming up behind us.

"Put your money where your mouth is, mister," I replied, and Oliver reached into his pockets, pulling out tokens with a cocky grin.

Another hour later, we were all out of tokens and I was exhausted, my feet aching from working last night and being on them for too long while playing Pac-Man.

"You all right?" Oliver asked, and I nodded tiredly.

"Just need to get off my feet," I said with a wince. "I think they're swollen."

"Why?" Trent asked, looking at me with his head tilted.

"Because sometimes the baby makes that happen," I explained.

Trent got very close to my stomach, putting a hand on it. "Don't do that, little sister. Don't hurt Mommy."

I couldn't help but smile. "Thanks, Trent."

"Did she listen?"

"I'm sure she did."

Trent patted my belly again. "Good girl."

Oliver looked down at us, and when I met his warm brown eyes, there were tears in them.

"Now I'm the one who should be asking you if you're okay," I teased gently.

"I'm perfect, too," he said, wiping his eyes with the back of his hand.

"Me, too," Trent piped up.

I giggled. "It seems like he never meets a stranger."

"Not a single one," Oliver agreed, laughing as we headed out of the arcade. Trent had pouted a little about leaving, but he didn't throw a fit. He really was a good kid.

Later that night, after I'd read Trent three stories before he finally went to sleep, I crawled into Oliver's bed, gasping at the luxuriousness of the soft sheets.

"Why don't I have these sheets?"

"Because you have been living in the guest house," Oliver said. "At least, until now."

I groaned in pleasure as I pulled the sheets and comforter over me. "Well, I want these sheets."

Oliver frowned. "These are your sheets."

My cheeks flushed pink. "Are you sure you want me to move in so quickly?"

"Yes," he said instantly.

"But Trent—"

"Trent loves you. He's already calling you mommy. I want you here with me, with us, Lex."

"I guess it would give your parents some time to reconnect," I mused. "Having me watch Trent instead."

"And it would give you two time to bond before the baby gets here." Oliver smiled. "It's perfect."

I thought about it for a long moment, biting my lip. It

wasn't like I was worried about moving in with Oliver, or even bonding with Trent. What I was really afraid of, well, it was hard to explain, even to myself.

"Something's wrong," Oliver pointed out, covering me with his body, pressing his forehead against mine. "What's wrong, baby?"

I swallowed hard, feeling tears threatening again. God, was I going to cry through this whole pregnancy?

"I'm afraid," I admitted softly.

"Afraid of what?"

"Of losing this," I said with a slight wave of my hand. "Of losing you, losing Trent. Losing all of this. Because well, I lost it before."

"That was because of my stupidity," Oliver said with a frown. "And I'll never be that stupid again, I promise you that."

I looked at him then leaned up to kiss him.

"You'd better not be," I muttered.

"Wouldn't dream of it."

I kissed him again, and when he guided himself inside me, I knew that this *was* perfect, just like I'd thought earlier.

Nothing and no one would ever take it from me again.

Perhaps fairy tales could come true.

Chapter 32

Oliver

Six Months Later

I paced around the back of the church, my palms sweating.

"Why are you so nervous?" my best man asked, and I let out a long breath.

"I don't know. What if she changes her mind? What if she runs? She ran the last time," I muttered.

"What, you think she's going to leave Trent and Daisy behind?" He chuckled, coming up behind me.

"I'm freaking out, Tristan. Isn't it your job to keep me from freaking out?"

"I'm trying," he said, still grinning.

"You think this is funny, don't you?" I grumbled as I fixed my tie for the thirtieth time.

"Hilarious," he admitted, snickering. "You're running around like a chicken with its head cut off, and it's still twenty minutes before the ceremony starts. It's going to be fine."

"So you don't think she's lacing up her running shoes?"

"Absolutely not. She loves you, Ollie. You and Lexie

have always been meant to be. This is just going to make it official."

I smiled and sat down, taking in a deep breath, letting it out through my nostrils. He was right. Everything was going to be okay.

Everything was perfect and it had been for the last six months.

Lexie had moved into my house, and we were renting out the cabin to Gillian, who wanted to be closer to the kids. She was a wonderful aunt and a huge help to Lex. She also watched Trent and Daisy for us during our date nights, which were frequent.

Lexie had gotten her job back at the grocery store because she said she was going nuts being home all the time. My grandmother was thrilled to have her.

Deep down I knew there was no way she would run from this but I couldn't help worrying about it. She ran on her wedding day before, but it was from an abusive dick— pun intended—who was now currently serving a year sentence in prison for his assault on Lexie.

Of course, Lexie and I had a few fights leading up to the wedding. Wedding planning was stressful, especially with two kids, and we still hadn't decided on a honeymoon trip.

But a few arguments and slammed doors wouldn't make her run, would it?

A knock sounded on the door, and I called for them to come in.

My heart pounded, hoping it wasn't someone telling me the bride was missing.

My father stood in the doorway, looking at me with wet eyes. "Oliver. You look sharp, son."

I sighed in relief. "Dad. Thank you." I smiled. "You look

pretty sharp yourself." His suit hid most of his beer belly and showed off his broad shoulders.

He chuckled. "Your mother thought so."

I wrinkled my nose. Ever since they'd gotten back together, they'd been publicly affectionate to each other in a way they never had before the separation, and it was taking some getting used to.

"How's Lex?" I asked, and he shrugged.

"Your mother is in the bridal room with her. Something about hair. You know I don't understand women speak."

I couldn't help but laugh. "No, Dad, you certainly don't."

Tristan stayed quiet. Although Lexie and my father's relationship had been repaired for the most part, Tristan wasn't so forgiving. It was understandable, at least to me, and my dad seemed to take it in stride.

"They should be ready soon," Dad said. He came over and hugged me tightly before he left the room.

Tristan released the breath he'd been holding, and I winced slightly.

"You all right?"

"I'm good," he said, giving me a slightly weak smile. "What about you? You over your crisis?"

"It wasn't a crisis," I muttered. Tristan squeezed my shoulder.

"Then let's take our places."

Tristan led me to the altar then clapped me on the shoulder before walking down the aisle to take his own place.

The priest smiled at me and I gave a weak smile back.

I couldn't wait to see Lexie.

My mother waved at me before waving Daisy's little

hand, and I waved back at them, smiling. Daisy had been such a sun ray in our lives.

She was babbly and happy, sleeping through the night at just a couple of weeks old. She adored Trent more than anything in the world, crawling to follow him around and mimicking him with noises.

Trent, on the other hand, was the world's most overprotective older brother, always right beside his little sister, always worried she might get hurt. They were adorable together, and Lexie had taken on the role of mother like she'd been born to play it. She'd redecorated the house to make it have a woman's touch, whatever that means.

Tristan had been right. Lexie would never run from Trent and Daisy, even if I thought she might run from me. I had to trust her. I had to keep trusting her because there was a time where I didn't, and it wrecked my life.

Everything had been terrible without Lexie, and now that she was back, I wasn't going to waste a moment.

Finally, the music started, and the groomsmen began ushering the bridesmaids down the aisle.

Gillian was the maid of honor, and a few other friends and family rounded out the bridal party. Krista and Raoul from the bar, and Clayton who sold me the place, were also included.

It seemed like the whole of Wagontown was there, filling up the pews. The place was packed full.

I waited patiently for Lexie to walk down the aisle, and when she did, my breath caught in my throat. She had her veil down so I couldn't make out her face, but her creamcolored dress had a plunging neckline that showed her cleavage, and it was tight across her hips, which had widened after having Daisy.

She looked unbelievable, and tears burned at the backs of my eyes.

When she arrived at the altar, I took her hand, pulling her to me, and lifted the veil.

Her green eyes were bright and clear. I was the only one crying, apparently. She smiled and reached up to thumb tears from my face I didn't even know had fallen.

"You big softie," she murmured in a low tone, and I chuckled.

"You just look so beautiful."

The priest started his speech, telling the audience that he was honored to be officiating our wedding, and I smiled at him. He was an old family friend who had actually married my parents, and though he was getting on in age, he was still a great speaker.

When it was time for the rings, Trent strolled down the aisle as if it was a catwalk in his little charcoal gray suit, and I couldn't help but grin ear to ear when he brought us the rings.

Lexie leaned down and kissed him on the cheek and he grinned up at her before going to sit with his grandmother. He promptly put Daisy on his lap, and she leaned back against him, comfortable as could be.

The vows went by in a flash. Soon enough, I was kissing Lexie as her husband and running outside while being pelted with bird seed that got in Lexie's hair and into my suit jacket pockets.

The limo was taking us right to the reception. We were eager to get the party started with our friends and family.

"I'm so glad I can drink," Lexie said, and I snorted out a laugh.

"That's the first thing you say as my wife?" I teased.

"You try being pregnant for nine months and then

breastfeeding for three," she pouted. "I think it's past time to have a glass of wine."

"Of course, baby," I crooned, kissing her neck.

She moaned. "Any way we can get this limo to park before we make it to the reception?"

"Probably not," I said mournfully, and Lexie giggled. "We have all night to consummate the marriage," I smiled, kissing her softly.

The Pig in the Poke was decked out for the event, with balloons and streamers everywhere, blown up pictures of Lexie and me when we were young, pictures of Lexie in her hospital bed after having Daisy. My favorite picture was one of Trent and Daisy after she was first born. Trent was looking down at her, smiling, as she looked up at him with wonder.

My heart ached at how much I loved everyone there, even including my father. I was still so angry that we had been forced apart by his actions, but perhaps we needed that time apart to figure ourselves out. Now we had a wonderful life together as a real family.

Lexie was on her third glass of champagne when she looked up at me with glassy eyes. "How are you, husband?"

"Not as tipsy as you, wife," I teased, and she smacked me playfully on the shoulder. I just laughed.

"Remember when we split that bottle of champagne out at Lover's Look?" she asked, giggling.

"I do. I remember you were *wild* that night," I murmured into her ear, pulling her close and kissing her temple.

"I was. So you remember what champagne does to me?"

My eyes widened. "Oh?"

"Oh, indeed. You're in for a hell of a wedding night," she joked.

Krista came over to congratulate us as Tristan called me over for a drink. I sipped the whiskey with a sigh.

"Been a long time since I've had whiskey," I said. "I gave it up for the most part after Lexie got pregnant."

"You're going to be a really good husband," Tristan said. "Don't know that I could do that."

I raised an eyebrow. "What, sacrifice for your wife?" I asked with a chuckle. "You thinking of making an honest woman out of Elena?"

He flushed a deep red. "We're still just dating," he mumbled, and I barked out a surprised laugh.

"Oh, so you admit you're dating now? Is it exclusive?"

"Yes," he said defensively.

"So she's your girlfriend."

"Please don't say that word," he mumbled, and I laughed again, clapping him on the shoulder.

"Congrats, buddy. You deserve happiness."

He smiled up at me, and I found myself feeling a wave of affection for my old friend. He could have treated me like a jerk for the rest of his life but he hadn't. He'd accepted my apology and we'd gone right back to being best friends.

By the time the reception was over, my head was spinning from the alcohol. Lexie was hanging on my arm, smiling, and flirting with me. I was ready to get the hell out of there.

We said goodbye to all our family and friends then kissed the kids before sending them off with Aunt Gillian.

As I helped Lexie out of her dress back at the hotel—which was a feat in itself, especially with our level of inebriation—I had a question to ask her.

"Where do you want to honeymoon?" She asked.

"Hawaii? The Bahamas? Paris?" I suggested.

She shook her head. "Nothing like that."

"Don't tell me you want to go somewhere cold," I groaned.

She laughed. "Nothing like that, either."

"Then where do you want to go?" I asked incredulously.

Finally, the buttons on the wedding dress cooperated and the dress slipped off her, leaving her bare. I'd already taken off my shirt and stood there in my slacks, looking her up and down hungrily.

"Wagontown," she said, and my eyes shot back up to her face.

"What?"

"I want to stay right here, with our kids and our family and friends. It's our home, and I wouldn't want to be anywhere else."

"Not exactly a normal honeymoon location," I told her, pressing a kiss to her lips.

She shrugged. "Maybe your folks can babysit so that we can have sex all over the house. Would that make it more like the expensive vacation that you wanted to plan?"

I grinned. "Budget-friendly alone-time. Sure. Why not?"

She giggled. "Then it's decided. A staycation it is."

I smiled and kissed her, knowing our happily ever after was finally beginning.

THE END

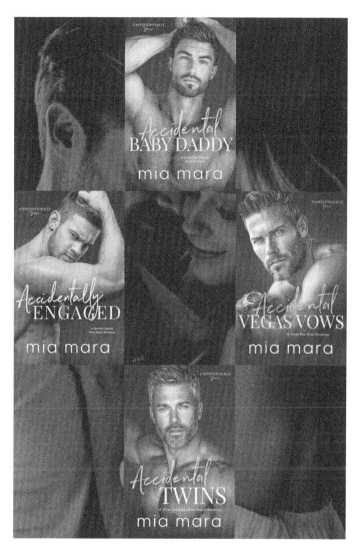

Unintentionally Yours Series

Get ready to fire up your kindle with these cinnamon-roll billionaires! When spicy, sugarcoated accidental engagements, marriages, and babies bring opposites together.

Each book follows the story of their own couple and are standalones with a very satisfying HEA.

Read the Unintentionally Yours series on Amazon:

Unintentionally Yours series page

Accidentally Engaged: A Fertility Doctor Next Door Romance (Hudson and Sophie)

Accidental Vegas Vows: A Silver Fox Boss Romance (Damien and Olivia)

Accidental Twins: A Silver Fox Dad's Best Friend Romance (Adrian and Ava)

Accidental Baby Daddy: A Single Dad Runaway Bride Romance (Oliver and Lexie)

Happy reading!

xx

Mia

Boulder Billionaires Series

Fire up your kindle with these four bossy billionaires from Colorado! These swoon-boats will impress, grovel and pleasure their way to a delicious HEA with their sassy woman. And they won't take no for an answer - not in the office and certainly not in the bedroom.

Each book follows the story of their own couple and are standalones with a very satisfying HEA. You'll also enjoy cameo appearances from your favorite characters throughout the series.

Read the Boulder Billionaires series on Amazon:

Boulder Billionaire series page

Big & Bossy: A Fake Engagement Second Chance Romance
(Jackson and Mandy)

Brute & Bossy: A Fake Relationship Opposites Attract Romance
(Wade and Raylene)

Beast & Bossy: A Fake Relationship Enemies to Lovers Romance
(Hunter and Lottie)

Bad & Bossy: A One Night Stand Secret Baby Romance
(Cole and Dana)

Happy reading!

xx

Mia

Made in the USA
Monee, IL
20 November 2024

70689259R00148